WINNING HI

A STORY OF FRESHMAN YEAR AT COLLEGE

EVERETT T. TOMLINSON

Edition : Culturea (Hérault, 34)
Contact : infos@culturea.fr
Print in Germany by Books on Demand
Design and layout : Derek Murphy
Layout : Reedsy (https://reedsy.com/)
ISBN : 9791041953721
Légal deposit : September 2023

Winning His "W"

A Story of Freshman Year at College

CHAPTER I

THE OPENING TERM

"I've got a letter from Peter John."

"What's the trouble with him? He ought to have been here yesterday or the day before."

"I'm afraid Peter John never'll be on time. He doesn't seem to have taken that in his course. He'd never pass an 'exam' in punctuality."

"What does he want?"

"The poor chap begs us to meet him at the station."

"What train?"

"The two-seventeen."

"Then we've no time to waste. Is he afraid he'll be lost?"

"He's afraid, all right."

"What's he afraid of?"

"Everything and everybody, I guess. Poor chap."

Will Phelps laughed good-naturedly as he spoke, and it was evident that his sympathy for "Peter John" was genuine. His friend and room-mate, Foster Bennett, was as sympathetic as he, though his manner was more quiet and his words were fewer; their fears for their friend were evidently based upon their own personal knowledge.

For four years the three young men had been classmates in the Sterling High School, and in the preceding June had graduated from its course of study, and all three had decided to enter Winthrop College. The entrance examinations had been successfully passed, and at the time when this story opens all had been duly registered as students in the incoming class of the college.

Foster Bennett and Will Phelps were to be room-mates, and for several days previous to the September day on which the conversation already recorded had taken place they had been in the little college town, arranging their various belongings in the room in Perry Hall, one of the best of all the dormitory buildings. The first assembling of the college students was to occur on the morrow, and then the real life upon which they were about to enter was to begin.

The two boys had come to Winthrop together, the parents of both having decided that it was better to throw the young students at once upon their own resources rather than to accompany them, reserving their visits for a later time when the first novelty of the new life would be gone.

And on this September day the novelty certainly was the most prominent element in the thoughts of both boys. The task of arranging their various belongings in their new rooms had kept both so busy that thoughts of the homes they had left were of necessity somewhat rare, and the vision of the family life in which they had been so vital a part had not as yet come to take the place in their minds which it soon would occupy.

At the hotel where they had been staying there were many other boys who were in a predicament not unlike their own, but the very fact that all were alike new to the life and its surroundings had made every one somewhat diffident and the warm friendships and cordial relations that soon were to be formed were as yet not begun.

Will Phelps and Foster Bennett, however, had been so completely taken up with their own immediate tasks that they had little thought for other things. At the time when this story opens their study room was ready for callers, as Will expressed it, and the adjoining sleeping rooms were in a fair way for occupancy. Indeed, the boys planned that very night to sleep in the dormitory, and the experience was looked forward to as one which they both would enjoy.

Will Phelps, a sturdy young fellow of eighteen, of medium height, with strong body and a bright, keen expression in his dark eyes, had been the most popular of all the boys in the high school from which he had recently graduated. Not over-fond of study, he had somewhat neglected his tasks until his final year, and though he had then begun to work more seriously, his late effort had not entirely atoned for the neglect of the preceding years. An only son and not rigidly trained in his home, he had not formed the habits of study which his more serious-minded room-mate, Foster Bennett, possessed. But almost every one who met the young student was drawn to him by the fascination of his winning ways, and realized at once the latent possibilities for good or ill that were his. His success would depend much upon his surroundings, and though Will was sublimely confident in his ability to meet and master whatever opposed him, it nevertheless had been a source of deep satisfaction to his father and mother that he was to room with his classmate, Foster Bennett, for Foster was of a much more sedate disposition than his friend. Taller than Will by three inches, as fond as he of certain athletic sports, still Foster was one whom enthusiasm never carried away nor impulse controlled. When people spoke of him they often used the word "steady" to describe him. Not so quick nor so brilliant as Will, he was not able to arouse the response which his room-mate seldom failed to elicit, nor was his promise in certain ways so great. Will might do brilliant things, but of Foster it was said that 'one always knew where to find him.' Naturally, the two boys in a measure complemented each other, and their friendship was strong and lasting.

Peter John Schenck—no one ever thought of referring to him by another term than "Peter John"—the third member of the high-school class to which reference has already been made, was a boy who every morning had driven into the little city of Sterling from his country home, and in his general appearance was decidedly unlike either of his classmates. The influences of his home had been of a different character from those which had surrounded his two friends. Not that the love for him had been less, but certain elements of refinement had been lacking and his familiarity with the ways of the world was much less. Besides, his father had been in humbler circumstances, and Peter John was to room in college in Leland Hall, one of the oldest of the dormitories, where the room rent was much less than in Perry Hall and more in accord with Peter John's pocket. In school he had been made the butt of many a joke, but his fund of good nature had never rebelled and his persistence was never broken. Tall, ungainly, his trousers seemed to be in a perpetual effort to withdraw as far as possible from his boots, while his hands and wrists apparently were continually striving to evade the extremities of his coat sleeves. His face was freckled, not the ordinary freckles produced by the heat of the sun, but huge splotches that in color almost matched his auburn-tinted hair—at least his sister was prone to declare that the color of his hair was "auburn," though his less reverent schoolmates were accustomed to refer to him as a "brick-top."

But Peter John was undeterred by the guying of his mates, and when he had first declared his intention to go to college his words had been received as a joke. But it was soon discovered that in whatever light they might be received by others, to Peter John himself they were the expression of a fixed purpose; and so it came to pass that he too had passed the entrance examinations and was duly enrolled as a member of the freshman class in Winthrop College.

When his determination had been accepted by his mates, some of them had made use of their opportunities to enlarge upon the perils that lay before him—perils for the most part from the terrible sophomores who were supposed to be going about seeking their prey with all the fierceness of a roaring lion. Peter John had listened to the marvelous tales that were poured into his ears, but so far as his expression of face was concerned, apparently they had been without effect. Nevertheless, deep in his heart Peter John had stored them all and his fear of the class above him had increased until at last just before he departed from home he had written to his friend Will Phelps informing him of his fears and begging that he and Foster would meet him at the station and protect him from the fierce onslaughts, which, he confessed, he expected would await him upon his arrival. This letter Will Phelps had found at the little post office when he made inquiries for his mail, and upon his return to his room it had provided the basis for the conversation already recorded.

"We'd better go right down to the station, then, Will," Foster had said.

"All right. Peter John will be in mortal terror if he shouldn't find us there. He probably believes the sophs will have a brass band and knives and guns and will be drawn up on the platform ready to grab him just the minute he steps off the car."

"Not quite so bad as that," laughed Foster. "But we'll have to help the poor chap out."

"Sure. Come on, then," called Will as he seized his cap and started toward the hallway.

"Hold on a minute. Wait till I lock the door."

"'Lock the door?' Not much! You mustn't do that."

"Why not?"

"It isn't polite."

"What are you talking about?" demanded Foster.

"Just what I'm telling you. Freshmen mustn't lock their doors, that's not the thing. The janitor told me not to, because the sophs will take it as a challenge to break it in. He said the college had to put sixty new locks this summer on the doors here in Perry."

"Looks as if something had happened for a fact," said Foster slowly, as he glanced at some huge cracks that were plainly visible in the panels. "Sure 't'll be safe?"

"It'll be all right. The janitor says so. Come on! Come on, or we'll be too late!"

The two boys ran swiftly down the stairway (their room was on the third floor of the dormitory) and soon were on the street which was directly in front of the building. As they walked rapidly in the direction of the station, which was a half-mile or more distant from the college buildings, the sight which greeted their eyes was one that stirred the very depths of their hearts. The very buildings themselves were impressive, some old and antiquated, dating back a century or more and venerable with age, and others new and beautiful, the recent gifts of some loyal alumni. From the huge clock in the tower of the chapel rang out the chimes which announced that the hour of two was come and gone. The beautifully kept grounds, the stately buildings, the very leaves on the huge elms that grew about the grounds were all impressive at the time to the boys to whom the entire picture was new.

In the wide street that led directly through the midst of the college buildings, were passing young men of their own age, some of whom would suddenly stop and grasp with fervor the hands of some students just returned from the long summer vacation. From the windows of the dormitories could be seen the faces of students who were leaning far out and shouting their words of greeting to friends on the street below. The September sun was warm and mellow, and as it found its way through the thick foliage it also cast fantastic shadows upon the grass that seemed to dance and leap in the very contagion of the young life that abounded on every side. The very air was almost electric and the high hills in the distance that shut in the valley and provided a framework for the handiwork of nature, lent an additional charm to which Will Phelps was unconsciously responding.

"I tell you, Foster, this is great! I'm glad I'm here!" he exclaimed.

"Are you?" replied Foster in his more subdued manner. "Well, I'm glad too."

The scene upon the platform of the station was as animated and inspiring as that about the college grounds. Groups of students were here awaiting the coming of friends, and yet their impatience was hidden by the enthusiasm of the moment. One group, consisting of twenty or more young men, particularly interested Will, for their noise and exuberance seemed to know no bounds. At last a young man, evidently a student though slightly older than the most in the group, approached them and said: "Here, you sophs! You're making too much noise. Children should be seen, not heard."

"All right, pop," responded one; and for a time the noise decreased. But it was not long before it broke forth afresh and became even more violent than before. Both Will and Foster were curiously watching the group; they almost instinctively looked upon them as natural enemies and yet were compelled to laugh at their antics.

"Here you, taxi-driver," suddenly called out one of the sophomores advancing from the midst of his classmates and approaching one of the cabs, a line of which were drawn up near the platform.

"Yes, sir. Yes, sir. Here you are! Here you are! This way!" responded a half-dozen of the taxi-drivers.

"Be still!" replied the young man solemnly to the noisy men. "Can't you see I'm engaged with John? Now, John, tell me honestly, are you free?"

"Yes, sir. Yes, sir. Take you anywhere ye say," responded the driver glibly.

"You're sure you're at liberty?"

"Yes, sir. Yes, sir."

"All right, then. I'm glad to hear it. I've a great respect for liberty. That's all I wanted to know; thank you," he added, politely bowing; then turning to his classmates he said: "I say, fellows, make it three for liberty!"

The cheers were given with a will, and then the leader added solemnly, "Let's make it three for our class, the best class that ever entered old Winthrop! Now then!"

These cheers also were loudly given, but they ceased abruptly when it was seen that the train, for whose coming they had been waiting, was now approaching.

CHAPTER II

PETER JOHN'S ARRIVAL

Before the rumbling train halted at the station, there was a rush of students toward it, all eager to welcome the incoming crowd, and every one apparently being desirous of being the first to greet his friends. Upon the platforms of the cars also crowds of students were to be seen, waving their hats in the air or standing with their traveling bags in their hands, all as eager as the boys at the station to be foremost in the reunion scene.

Will Phelps and his room-mate stood a little back from the assembly and watched the proceedings with an interest which neither could conceal. It was all so stimulating, this animation and bustle and manifest eagerness in renewing the college life, and to feel that they too were to have a share in the possessions of these young men, scarcely one of whom was known to them personally, was in itself sufficient to quicken their pulses and arouse all the dormant forces of their nature. The train was a long one and yet from every car came pouring forth the stream of students and the excitement continued for several minutes.

Suddenly a shout went up from the crowd and there was a rush of students toward the rear car. "There's Baker! Good old Sam! Hurrah for the captain!" were among the cries that could be heard as the students surged toward the platform, from which a sturdy young man could be seen descending, apparently unmindful of the interest his coming had aroused and striving to be indifferent to the cheers that greeted his arrival.

Will Phelps and Foster Bennett almost unconsciously moved with the throng though they were not fully aware of the cause of the sudden interest of the students. "It may be that he's the captain of the football team," said Will in a low voice to his companion. "At any rate the captain's name is Baker and probably this is the man."

Foster nodded his head but made no other reply as he stood watching the young man as he stepped down from the platform. There could be no question as to who he was, for the conquering hero was writ large upon his powerful frame and the universal deference of the student body could be accounted for only by the fact that a leader in Winthrop had arrived.

"Look there, Will," said Foster suddenly. "There's Peter John."

"Where?"

"Right behind Baker. Just coming out of the door. See him?"

"Yes," responded Will as he obtained a glimpse of his classmate just as he was emerging from the doorway. Travel-stained, his hat pushed back on his head, his eyes wildly staring about at the crowd, a huge carpet-bag in his hand, his appearance certainly would have attracted the attention of the spectators had it not been that their interest was apparently centered in the mighty captain of the football team and they had no thought for any one else.

Just as Baker stepped down, Peter John emerged from the car directly behind the captain, and a cheer louder than any that before had been given rose from the assembly.

Poor Peter John! Nervous and excited, conscious only of himself and his strange surroundings, the startled freshman had no other thought than that the cheers were meant for him and doubtless were intended as a war cry from those enemies of whom he had heard such marvelous tales—the sophomores. Wild-eyed, for a moment he seemed to be well-nigh paralyzed. He stood motionless and gazed out at the surging mass of students almost as if he were minded to turn back into the car and escape from the threatening peril. But the pressure from behind was too strong to permit him to carry out his intention and he was compelled to move forward. As yet he had not seen his two waiting friends and his feeling of utter loneliness swept over him afresh. From the lowest step he was about to move when another mighty shout went up from the assembly and Peter John looked helplessly about him as if he were convinced that his doom was sealed and for him there was to be no escape.

Suddenly he darted from the midst of the crowd, sending two or three young men who chanced to be in his way sprawling, and with his quaint carpet-bag still tightly grasped in his hand fled directly back over the railway ties. He had not gone far before his flight was perceived and a shout of laughter and derision arose. Even the mighty Baker was ignored in the fresh excitement and instantly a crowd of students started in pursuit of the fleeing freshman.

"Hi, there! Stop, freshman! Wait a minute; we'll help carry your bag! Look at the sprinter! Going home? Good-bye! Good-bye!" were among the derisive cries that he heard. There could be no mistake, the attention of the entire student body was upon him, he was convinced, and his speed increased. His long legs, his flying coat tails, his flapping carpet-bag, indeed his entire appearance was such that shrieks of laughter arose from his pursuers, but Peter John never once glanced behind him. Every fresh call served to increase his terror. Life, liberty, and the pursuit of happiness were about to be taken from him and his sole hope depended upon his own exertions. It was do or die, and Peter John preferred the former.

In a brief time the good-natured crowd abandoned its pursuit, and Peter John Schenck was left to continue his lonely flight. Will Phelps and Foster Bennett had joined in the laughter at first, for the ridiculous flight of their classmate was well-nigh irresistible; but when it soon became apparent that Peter John's terror was real and that he firmly believed the entire college was in swift pursuit of him, their attitude changed.

"It's too bad, Will," said Foster. "The poor chap is scared almost to death."

"We can't help it. He'll have to learn some things, if not others," laughed Will.

"They're coming back," suggested Foster, as the pursuit was abandoned and the students laughing boisterously returned to the station.

Peter John, however, was still fleeing and his long strides and his wildly flapping carpet-bag could be distinctly seen as the frightened freshman sped up the track. The body of students, however, had now turned into the street that led back to the college grounds, and apparently Peter John's wild flight was already forgotten.

"We must go after him," said Foster thoughtfully.

"Oh, leave him alone," replied Will. "He'll come back all right."

"You go up to the room and I'll go and look him up."

"Not much! If you go, then I go too! I may be the next victim and I don't intend to be offered up alone. Come on, or he'll be clear back in Sterling before we find him."

Will laughed as he spoke, and at once the two boys started up the track in the direction in which their classmate had fled. He could not be seen now for a bend in the road had concealed him from sight, and for a time his two friends did not dare to run, being fearful that they too might attract an undue amount of attention and bring upon themselves the many ills from which they were striving to save their friend.

Apparently their departure from the station had not drawn the attention of any one, and, as they became convinced that they were not being followed, their own speed increased until they too had passed the bend in the road, when they began to run swiftly. Nothing could be seen of Peter John, and when they had gone a considerable distance Will Phelps stopped and whistled.

At first there was no response, but when the signal had been thrice repeated both boys heard the voice of their friend apparently coming from behind the bushes growing on the bank directly beside them.

"All alone, Will?" called Peter John timidly.

"Yes. Yes. Where are you, Peter John?" responded Will, peering about him, but as yet unable to determine where his friend was hiding.

"Here I am."

"Where's that?"

"Right here."

"Come out here where we are. Stand up like a little man and be counted."

"Sure nobody's with you?"

"Foster's here, that's all."

Slowly Peter John arose from his hiding-place and peered anxiously about him. "It's all right. Come on!" called Will encouragingly. Thus bidden, Peter John stepped forth, still holding tightly in his grasp his precious carpet-bag. Will Phelps did not even laugh nor did he have any inclination to do so as he perceived how genuine was the suffering of the terrified boy.

"You needn't be afraid now, Peter John," he said soothingly. "You're all right."

"That was a close call."

"Call for what?" demanded Foster sharply. Will turned and looked in surprise at his room-mate, for the tone of his voice was very unlike that which he had used when he had insisted that they should go to the aid of their classmate.

"I tell you they were after me!" said Peter John, wiping his brow with a huge handkerchief as he spoke."Who were after you?" demanded Foster still more sharply.

"The sophomores."

"Don't you believe it!"

"Why, they'd have got me if I hadn't put in my prettiest."

"Nobody would have paid any attention to you if you hadn't run. You drew it all on yourself and have no one else to blame."

"Guess you weren't there when I landed! They gave such a yell when I started from the cars as I never heard before in all my born days."

"Did you think they were yelling for you?"

"Of course I did. I knew they'd be waiting for me."

"Peter John, you've made a fool of yourself. There wasn't a soul there except Will and me that knew there was such a fellow in all the world as Peter John Schenck. Everybody in college will know it now, though."

"What made 'em yell so, then?" demanded Peter John.

"They weren't yelling for you at all. They were cheering for Baker, the captain of the football team. He was just ahead of you."

"They were?"

"That's what I said." Foster smiled slightly as he spoke, for the expression upon the face of Peter John was a study. Consternation, incredulity, and partial unbelief in what Foster had said were all expressed there, and his entire attitude was so indescribably ludicrous as almost to be pathetic."Swan! I didn't know that," he said at last slowly.

"Well, you know it now."

"What shall I do?"

"'Do'? Do nothing. Just attend to your own business and let everything else go."

"I thought I was attending to my own business," said Peter John woefully.

"Oh, well, never mind, Peter John," broke in Will with a laugh. "It's all over now and no bones broken."

"I wish it was all over," said Foster in a low voice to Will.

"I wish it was too. He'll be the center of interest by to-morrow. And really, Foster, it did beat anything I ever saw."

Foster Bennett smiled but made no reply, and together the three boys began to retrace their way to the station. Peter John evidently was somewhat crestfallen and seldom spoke. At the station no students were seen, and the trio at once started up the street toward the college.

"I suppose my things are in my room," Peter John ventured to suggest.

"Yes, they're there all right. I went over this morning to see about them."

"Thank you. I'll be pretty busy for the rest of the days I take it."

"That won't do you any harm. You can come over and sleep on the couch in our room to-night if you would like to," suggested Foster.

"Are you all settled?""Pretty much. Enough so that we can make room for you. There's always room for one more, you know." Foster spoke pleasantly and Peter John was quick to respond. They were now near the college grounds, however, and the interest of Peter John was quickly taken up in his surroundings. Both Will and Foster were familiar with the name of every building by this time, and their residence of three days in the college town had already given to them a sense of part possession, and they glibly explained to their classmate the name and use of each building as they passed it until at last they halted before Leland Hall, where Peter John was to have his room.

"I'd like to know who's to be my room-mate," he said as all three turned into the low entry and began to mount the worn stairway.

"Probably he's thinking of the same thing too," laughed Will. "Here you are," he added as he stopped before the door of a room on the third floor. "Yours is twenty-six, isn't it?"

"Yes."

"Well, here it is."

"Come on in, fellows," urged Peter John, opening the door as he spoke, and all three found themselves in the presence of a young man of their own age, who glanced quickly up from the box which he was unpacking as they entered.

CHAPTER III

NEW FRIENDS AND NEW EXPERIENCES

"One of you, I fancy, is Schenck, who is to room here with me. I haven't the remotest idea which one of you is the man, but whichever it is I'm glad to see him."

The young man laughed heartily as he spoke, and all three of the freshmen laughed in response so contagious was his good nature. But his appearance was even more striking than his words, for he stood before them like a young giant. He was at least six feet and three inches in height, his shoulders were so broad that they made the very doorway appear narrow, and as he stood before them without his coat and with his shirt sleeves rolled back over his arms, the great knots of muscles could be plainly seen. Altogether he presented a most impressive sight, and his young classmates were duly impressed by his huge size and evident physical strength.

"I'm Schenck," said Peter John, after a momentary hesitation.

"Glad to see you," exclaimed the young giant, stepping forward and grasping his room-mate's hand in such a manner as to make Peter John wince. "You know what my name is, I suppose. I'm Hawley. 'Cupe' Hawley they called me in school because I was such a dainty and delicate little specimen." And again his laughter broke forth. "Friends of yours, Schenck?" he added, as he glanced inquiringly at the two companions of his room-mate.

Will Phelps and Foster Bennett were at once introduced, and warmly greeted their classmate.

"Sorry I can't offer you any seats, fellows," said Hawley, still laughing, though there was no apparent cause for his enjoyment. "Haven't got everything unpacked yet; but if you'll just wait a minute we'll find something for you to sit on."

"We'll help you," said Will Phelps, at once laying aside his coat.

In their room he and Foster had done but little of the labor required in unpacking their belongings, for neither had been accustomed to such tasks in the homes from which they had come. Their fathers both were well-to-do and it had not occurred to either of the boys that the manual labor in settling their room was something to be expected of them. For a moment Foster glanced quizzically at his friend as if he was puzzled to account for his unexpected proffer, but knowing Will's impulsiveness as he did he was quick to respond, and in a brief time the few belongings of Peter John and his room-mate were unpacked and the beds were set up, the shades at the windows, and the few scanty belongings all arranged.

"I didn't bring a carpet. Did you?" inquired Hawley of Schenck.

"No," replied Peter John.

"We can get along without one. I haven't any money to spare, and carpets are luxuries anyway. If we feel like it we can buy one afterwards. They're dangerous things though," and Hawley laughed as he spoke. "My doctor says they're the worst sources of contagion in the world, and whatever else I do I must be careful of my health." Again the laugh of the young giant rang out, and in its contagion all three of his classmates joined.

And yet as Will Phelps glanced about the room its appearance was pitifully bare. The furniture was of the plainest, the walls were bare of pictures, there were none of the numerous pillows and other tokens of the warm regard of friends that had accompanied himself and his room-mate into the new life upon which they had entered. Apparently, however, Hawley was as delighted over his surroundings as he and Foster over theirs, perhaps even more, and Will was thoughtful for a moment as he silently watched his newly made friend.

"How did you happen to come to Winthrop?" he inquired at last when the task of settling the room was measurably complete and all four had seated themselves on the rude wooden chairs which made up most of the furnishings of the room.

"I didn't 'happen' to come." Somehow everything appeared to be a source of enjoyment to Hawley, and questions or remarks were alike greeted with a laugh.

"What made you, then?"

"Isn't Winthrop the best college in the United States?" demanded Hawley.

"Yes, or at least that's what my father thinks. He graduated here and it may be that his opinion is a little prejudiced. Is that why you came?"

"Partly." Again Hawley laughed and closed one eye as he spoke.

"I can give a guess what the other reason was," said Foster."What was it?"

"Football."

Hawley laughed loudly this time as he replied, "You're 'a very Daniel come to judgment.' That's from the 'Merchant of Venice,' isn't it? Well, if it is, it's about all I remember of my English course. Well, I'll be honest with you. I did see Baker this summer, and he set before me the advantages of coming to Winthrop in such a way that I couldn't very well say no. And I didn't, so here I am."

"Did he offer to pay you?" demanded Peter John.

"Did he offer what?" demanded Hawley.

Somewhat abashed Peter John did not repeat his question, and his room-mate at once turned the conversation into other lines. "We had a pretty good football team in the academy where I fitted for college, and there were several colleges, or at least the football men of the college, who seemed to be quite willing that some of our fellows should go to them. We had a half-back who was a dandy! His name was Patrick O'Hara, and he passed better in football than he did in any other subject in the course." And Hawley stopped to laugh at the recollection of his former fellow-student. "Pat wasn't very much of a hand to study, and when one of the men from White College suggested to him that he should come there, why Pat was delighted. 'What studies will you take?' asked the fellow, for you see he knew without being told that Pat wouldn't be valedictorian of his class whatever other honor he might take, and he was trying to make it easy for him. 'Well,' said Pat, "bedad, an' if it's all th' same t' yez, I'm thinkin' I'll just be afther takin' a bit o' the spellin' an' perhaps a bit o' figurin'. How do thot be afther suitin' yez'?"

All the boys joined in the laugh with which Hawley related the story, and Will Phelps said, "Where did Pat go?"

"Well," said Hawley slowly, "he has gone to White College."

"Do you mean to say he has entered there?" demanded Will.

"That's what they tell me, though I've a notion he'll come out the same door he went in, and he won't tarry long either. Probably soon after the season ends."

"But we play White College. It's one of our nearest rivals," suggested Will. "But then," he added, "that's just like them. They never do a thing on the square anyway!"

Hawley pursed his lips as if he was about to whistle, but he did not speak though his eyes twinkled with merriment as if Will's statement somehow was hugely enjoyed by him. Foster Bennett noticing the expression on Hawley's face, also laughed, but he did not reply to his room-mate's very positive declaration. There were some things which Will could not understand, for with his intense and impulsive disposition the one thing which impressed him at the time was capable of only one interpretation. His confidence in Winthrop and his dislike of its rival college were therefore only what were to be expected of his friend.

"Obliged to you, fellows," said Hawley, as Will Phelps and Foster Bennett rose to depart. "Come in and see us often.""You'll see enough of us from now on," responded Will as he and his room-mate departed.

As the two passed out into the street and returned to their own room Foster said, "It's pretty bare there in Leland, isn't it, Will?"

"Yes. They both seem to be happy though."

"Not much like our room."

"No. But then, Foster, you see they don't know the difference."

Foster smiled but made no response, and Will continued. "You see everything in this world is relative. A man doesn't miss what he never had, does he?"

"Perhaps not."

"Now look here, Foster. Do you think a blind man suffers because he can't see? I mean a man who was born blind, of course."

"What then?"

"Why, the man I'm sorry for is the one that could see once and has lost his sight. He knows, let me tell you, what he's lost. But the other man doesn't appreciate it. He never could see, so he couldn't lose his sight, could he? Tell me that."

"So you wouldn't do anything to help him?"

"I didn't say that. I didn't say that at all. All I say is that the fellow I'm sorry for is the one who has had and lost, not the one who never had. Now look at Peter John, and Hawley. Their room isn't so good as ours, but it probably is just as good as they expected, or have been used to, so they don't suffer any.""And if you and I had to put up with their room—"

"Why, we'd feel it."

"It's a mighty comfortable way of looking at things, that's all I have to say."

"But it's the true way," said Will glibly. "There's one thing I'm mighty glad of for Peter John's sake."

"What is it?"

"That he rooms with Hawley. I don't believe the sophs will bother him very much."

"Not when Hawley's on hand."

"You think they will when he's not?"

"Yes, sir, I do. Peter John just invites them. It stands right out on his face."

"Sort of a standing invitation, so to speak?" laughed Will Phelps. "Well, for my part, I hope he won't be too fresh. There's everything in that, you know."

"And therefore we'll go scot free?"

"Well, Hawley is a great fellow anyway; and I'm glad he's in our class."

"He's big, anyway."

"That's what I said."

"No you didn't, you said great."

"Same thing."

"Not much. A man can be big without being great, can't he? Caesar and Napoleon were not big men, but I think you'd sum up that they were great.""Great butchers, if that's what you mean. You always spin it out too fine for me, Foster."

Foster Bennett laughed and both boys entered their room to prepare for dinner. They still were taking their meals at the hotel, as their boarding-place had not been selected. In the thoughts of both it was a selection of too much importance to be made hastily, and they were therefore waiting until they became more familiar with the details of their new life.

It was all novel and interesting, and on the following day the first class meeting was held. A dignified junior presided at the meeting, and after explaining what was expected and that the class officers to be selected were to serve only for a month, when it was thought that the members of the class would have become sufficiently acquainted with one another to enable them to act with becoming wisdom, he called for nominations for class president.

Peter John Schenck immediately arose and said, "I nominate Hawley."

The nomination was seconded, and there were calls for Hawley to step to the platform and stand where all the class could see him. The young giant obediently advanced and taking his place beside Spencer, who also was nominated for the office, awaited the verdict. There were cheers when it was announced that Hawley had won, and the junior then called for nominations for secretary and treasurer.

Again Peter John arose to the occasion and said, "I nominate Phelps."Will's face flushed scarlet at the unexpected words but his room-mate at once had seconded the nomination, and he was compelled to advance to the platform and stand beside Farmer and McVey, whose names were also presented for the same office. There was some confusion for a time, but quiet was restored when the result of the ballot was announced.

CHAPTER IV

A CLOUD OF WITNESSES

Will Phelps had been elected temporary secretary and treasurer of his class, the choice having been made chiefly because his appearance, as he stood on the platform, pleased his classmates, and not because of any general acquaintance that had been formed. And yet his election had brought him at once into a certain prominence, and doubtless Will was duly appreciative of the honor bestowed upon him.

The member of the junior class to whom had been entrusted the organizing of the freshmen now rose to give some general words of advice before the meeting was adjourned. "There are some things in college," he was saying, "that have the force of laws. Some of them will appear foolish to you, it may be, and yet it will be more foolish to disregard them. For example, freshmen are not expected to go up to the hotel parlors in the evening, it would be decidedly better for them not to display on their caps or jersey the letters or numerals of the schools from which they have come, and they must not tack their cards on the doors of their rooms." Walker, the junior, continued his directions until he thought he had covered most of the details of the life upon which the incoming class was entering, but his remarks were not completed when Peter John Schenck arose from his seat and stood facing the president. There was a momentary pause as Walker ceased speaking, and the eyes of all the class were turned toward Peter John.

After due deliberation, Peter John said in a loud voice, "Mr. President, I move that we adjourn."

The hush that followed was broken by a loud laugh which had been started by Walker himself. Peter John, however, glanced about the room as if he was unable to perceive what it was that had caused the outbreak. Apparently unabashed, he again turned to the class president and said, "Isn't a motion to adjourn always in order, Mr. President? If it is, then I repeat my former motion. I move that we adjourn."

Hawley was too good-natured to treat the interruption as it deserved, so he said, "Is the motion seconded?"

Apparently it was not, and still unabashed, Peter John again took his seat while Walker resumed his remarks.

"I don't know that I have anything more to say, only to tell you fellows to be careful. College traditions and customs have all the force of laws, and though some of them may seem to be foolish, still I believe in the main they help to make the life here what it is, and that's what you all want to get. If you have any questions to ask, don't be afraid to come to me with them, or to any of the juniors, and you'll be given all we know, which, though I can promise you it may not be much, still may be just a little more than you know. Or, perhaps, some of you," he added, glancing quizzically in the direction of Peter John Schenck as he spoke.

When Walker departed from the room, Peter John was again the first to arise. "I move we adjourn," he said in a loud voice.

"Second the motion," said Foster Bennett quickly. The motion was put and instantly carried, and the class passed out from the room.

"It was anything to shut up Peter John," Foster explained to Will as he joined his room-mate. "Did you ever see the like?"

"I never did," laughed Will. "I feel almost guilty to be acting as secretary for the class. If we had ten other offices to vote upon, I believe Peter John would have made the first nomination for every one."

"He certainly is the freshest freshman in the whole bunch."

"Yes, he doesn't know enough to know that he doesn't know, and that's about as far down as a fellow can go in his ignorance, you know."

"What shall we do for him?"

"Nothing."

"But he'll have trouble."

"Sure."

"I'd hate to see him catch it too hard."

"You can't save him, Foster. He's got to learn his lesson. The idea of his being on his feet so much to-day."

"Well, he helped us to some good officers anyway, I'll say that much for him," laughed Foster. "But if he made such an impression on our class, what'll he do for the sophomores?"

"You'd better be thinking about what they'll do for him."Walker now joined the two boys, introducing himself to each, and accompanying them to their room, where he entered and took a seat at their invitation. He was a fine-looking young man and of most agreeable manners, so that soon both Will and Foster were delighted with him personally and appreciative of the honor of the visit from their visitor.

"No," Walker was saying, "the hazing doesn't amount to anything much in Winthrop. It's nothing more than a little good-natured 'horse play' for the most part. Of course, once in a while a fellow gets a little more attention than the rest of the class; but as a rule it's his own fault. You have a classmate that'll be very popular with the sophs, if he doesn't look out," he added with a laugh.

"Who's that?" inquired Will, with a wink at his room-mate.

"The chap that was on his feet so much in the class meeting this afternoon."

"We were just talking about him," said Foster quickly. "You know he fitted at the same school where we did, and naturally we want to lend him a hand when we can. What had we better do?"

"Nothing."

"What do you mean?"

"Just what I say. You can't do much for such a fellow; he has to learn it all for himself. The trouble is that he doesn't know how much or what he's got to learn yet. You can't do much for such a—"

Walker stopped abruptly as Peter John himself entered the room. His face was beaming, and as he removed his hat his stiff red hair seemed almost to rise on his head. "Well, fellows," he said, "we did things up brown this afternoon, didn't we?"

"You did too much," said Walker quietly.

"Haven't I as good a right as anybody to make a motion?" demanded Peter John hotly.

"You have as much right, but you don't want always to take all your rights, you know."

"Why not? I'll stand up for my rights every time. Now, I don't believe a word of what you said this afternoon."

"You're complimentary; but you're under no obligations to believe me," laughed Walker.

"I don't mean just that. What I mean is that I'd like to see the sophomore who'd tell me what I could wear or what I couldn't; or where I could go and where I couldn't. He hasn't anything to say about that."

"He thinks he has," suggested Walker quietly.

"I don't care what he thinks. I know my rights, and I intend to stand up for them too!"

"Is that why you were running up the railroad track the day when you came to Winthrop?" demanded Will Phelps.

"Never you mind about that!" retorted Peter John in nowise abashed. "That was when I didn't know as much as I do now."

"Three or four days will do great things for a fellow," remarked Walker dryly.

"Yes, sir, that's so. You're right about that," acknowledged Peter John graciously. "Say, fellows, what are you going to do about these Greek letter societies?" he inquired abruptly, turning to his two classmates as he spoke.Both Will Phelps and Foster Bennett glanced uneasily at Walker, but the junior only smiled and made no response. It was apparent though that the topic Peter John had broached was one upon which all three had been conferring.

"We haven't done anything as yet," said Foster.

"Neither have I," acknowledged Peter John. "I thought I'd take my time before I decided which one I'd join. I suppose I'll have to write home to pa, but he won't know as much about it as I do."

"We live and learn," said Walker as he rose to depart. "I'll see you to-night?" he inquired of Will and Foster as he stopped for a moment in the doorway. Will glanced questioningly at his room-mate and then said: "Thank you, Walker. We'll be very glad to come."

"Where you going? What did he want?" demanded Peter John when Walker was gone.

"It was something personal," said Foster. "Walker thinks you'll have to walk the chalk line, Peter John, or you'll have trouble with the sophs."

"He does, does he? Well, I'll show him. I'd like to know what right they've got to tell me what to do. I'll do as I please! My chum—"

It was instantly plain to the boys now the cause for this sudden and strange change in Peter John's attitude. He was relying upon the prowess of Hawley to protect him now and apparently was confident that he would not be molested since he roomed with the young giant whose name already was known throughout the college and from whom such great things were expected for the football team.

"Don't depend too much upon Hawley! He can't be everywhere, remember," said Foster warningly.

"I'll show 'em, if they come near me!" retorted Peter John as he departed.

For several days the college life went on quietly and the boys were becoming somewhat accustomed to their new surroundings. There had been a "sweater rush" between the two lower classes, in which Hawley had been entrusted with the precious sweater, and, surrounded by his classmates, successfully defended it against the onslaught of the sophomores. The struggle had been severe but in good part, and the worst results had been some torn clothing and bruised faces. The freshmen wore upon their arms a strip of white cloth to enable them to distinguish their own comrades, and great was their elation when after the time limit had expired, it was discovered that the coveted sweater was unharmed. The strength of Hawley had been as the strength of ten and his praises were in every mouth.

Into this struggle Will Phelps had thrown himself with all his might, and when he joyfully emerged from the struggling mass of humanity gathered about Hawley his rejoicing was great and his cheers for the class were among the loudest.

On the border of the crowd he had perceived Peter John, but his classmate displayed no evidence of the recent struggle and Will was about to question him, when Peter John himself said, "Come over to my room to-night, Will."

"All right." Will Phelps had promised readily, and then the matter departed from his mind as he rushed about among his classmates.That evening he suddenly glanced up from the book he was studying and said to his room-mate: "Foster, I agreed to go over to Peter John's room to-night. Want to go?"

"Can't say that I'm pining for it. What does he want?"

"I don't know. He seemed to be very much in earnest about it, though."

"Is it much nearer from here to his room than it is from his room to ours? If he wanted to see you so much, why didn't he come over here?"

"That isn't Peter John's way," laughed Will. "I promised to go, so I think I'll run over for a minute. I'll be back pretty soon."

"If you need me let me know," called Foster as Will departed, and he then at once resumed his task.

Will Phelps ran across the campus to Leland Hall, and as he turned in at the dimly lighted hall the contrast between his own surroundings and those in which he now found himself was for the moment almost painful. The stone step at the entrance had been worn away by the passing of boyish feet over it for more than a century. For a moment there flashed into his mind the thought of the eager lives that there had been trained and long since had passed over into the land beyond. Will himself was the fourth generation in direct descent in his own family to enter Winthrop, and as he now passed slowly up the rough, narrow, and worn stairway, he found himself thinking of his own father and grandfather and great-grandfather, all of whom doubtless had many a time been in the very same hallway where he himself then was. Even then from far down the street came the sounds of song and laughter of some passing body of students and the faint sound he could hear was for the moment almost like the echo of long past days. The very hall seemed to echo also with the footfalls of students who had long since completed their course and passed on. He was surrounded by a cloud of witnesses.

Suddenly from the floor above him came the sound of noisy shouts and shrieks of laughter. The vision of other days and other men instantly departed, and the full force of the appeal of the present swept over him. Bounding up the steps, two at a time, he swiftly came to the third floor and then stopped abruptly as the shouts were redoubled and evidently came from Peter John Schenck's room.

For a moment Will hesitated, almost tempted to turn back, but his feeling of curiosity was strong and resolutely he advanced and rapped upon the door. This was quickly opened and Will stepped inside the room. The door had instantly been closed and bolted behind him, but Will was hardly aware of that so interested was he in the sight upon which he gazed in the room which was filled with a noisy group of students.

CHAPTER V

UNSOUGHT ATTENTIONS

One glance about him had been sufficient to convince Will Phelps that his classmates were suffering from a visit of the sophomores, a dozen or more of whom he recognized as being in the room. He looked quickly behind him at the door, but this already had been closed and three of the stalwart sophomores were standing with their backs against it, the others being stationed at different points about the room. In the center stood Mott, a lusty sophomore whom he had frequently seen and whose general bearing he had intensely disliked, for his face bore the unmistakable traces of dissipation and his bearing was that of a rowdy. The fact that Mott had secured a high position among the college athletes had in a measure made amends for his low tendencies of life in the eyes of his thoughtless mates, but though he was by nature somewhat of a leader still his personal popularity was low, and it was only his physical prowess that gave him any standing.

Seated upon one end of his study table was Hawley, his face beaming with good nature and smiling broadly as he faced the assembly in the room. In one corner Peter John was standing, his back against the wall and in his hands was one of the heavy wooden chairs which he was grasping by the rounds. Even in the somewhat dim light Will could see that the great splotches of red on Peter John's face appeared to be larger and of a more fiery tint than usual, and his coarse red hair fairly stood on end. There was an expression of mingled terror and wild, almost ungovernable, rage on his face, and Will knew what that portended at that time. A brief silence had followed Will's entrance, and Mott had turned to some of his comrades and a meaning smile appeared for a moment on his face as he perceived who the new-comer was. In a moment, however, the tense stillness of the room returned, and Mott, turning to Peter John, said:

"Now, then, freshman, are you ready?"

"I'll brain the first man that comes near me! Don't you lay a finger on me or I'll break your head! This is my room and I'll have you understand that you can't play any of your dirty tricks on me!"

Peter John's voice rose almost to a shriek, and lifting the chair he gazed menacingly at Mott, almost as if he was minded to rush upon him. Hawley laughed as his room-mate spoke, but Will's face became pale and he could almost hear the beating of his own heart, so intensely excited was he. He understood Peter John's disposition better than any of those who were in the room, and his fear of what might follow was great.

"We'll give you one more chance," said Mott slowly.

"I don't want any more chances. I want you to get out of this room! I didn't ask you to come! You've no right here!" shouted Peter John.

"You didn't have to ask us," retorted Mott. "We came because you need us and for the good of the college. Come, freshman, do what I tell you."

"Don't you come near—" began Peter John, but the sentence was not completed. At some unseen signal a half-dozen sprang upon him. Before he could bring down the chair which he still was holding above his head he was suddenly seized by his adversaries, the chair was wrenched from his hands, he was thrown heavily to the floor, and in a moment his hands and feet were fast bound with cords, and he was a helpless prisoner. Still he did not cease his struggling, but as he twisted and writhed he only drew the cords more tightly and made his own helplessness more apparent.

"I know who you are!" he shrieked. "I'll report you, every one! I'll give the whole list of your names to the president! I'll have you arrested! I'll put you in jail! You're a lot of thieves and low-down scoundrels! I'll have you put where you won't abuse anybody any more!" Peter John's voice rose with every fresh threat until at last it almost broke in a sob. He was almost beside himself, and Will Phelps, though he shared in the anger of his classmate, was rejoiced that he was helpless and could not do what his desperation prompted.

"Tie your handkerchief over his mouth, Hines," said Mott to one of his companions. "We must hush the infant's wailings or he'll have the whole of Winthrop up here. He seems to have some language besides that of the ordinary 'infant crying in the night'."

At Mott's direction Hines and two of his classmates at once securely bound a handkerchief about Peter John's face, a task that was not accomplished without a desperate struggle.

"Now then, since he seems to be quieted," said Mott at last, when his bidding had been done, "we'll turn to the other part of the program. Here, you freshman," he added, turning to Will Phelps as he spoke, "step up here and take your seat beside your classmate."

For an instant Will hesitated. The sight of Peter John roused every instinct of combativeness which he possessed, and that was by no means small, but a laugh from Hawley restored a measure of self-possession, and quietly and without a word he seated himself on the table by the side of his friend.

"Good! That's the way to do it! Now then, Hawley," said Mott, "you've got to get rid of that eternal grin of yours. Wipe that smile off your face and throw it out of the window."

Hawley laughed aloud as he said, "I've been trying to get rid of it for nineteen years, but I haven't succeeded yet. If you fellows will show me how to do it I'll be yours truly now and for evermore."

Some of the sophomores laughed, but Mott glared angrily at them as he said, "Quit that!" Then turning again to Hawley he said, "Oh, we'll help you all right enough. Just do as I tell you!"

"How shall I do it?"

"Take your handkerchief and wipe that smile off your face and throw it out of the window as I tell you."

Hawley drew a huge handkerchief from his pocket with which he vigorously rubbed his face, and then going soberly to the window pretended to throw something out; but when he returned to his seat his laughter became uncontrollable and he broke forth into a loud guffaw, in which some of the assembly joined.

At Mott's rebuke the laughter ceased, and then he said again to Hawley, "That won't do, freshman. You're not rid of it yet. Try it again!"

Six times the huge and good-natured freshman was compelled to repeat his senseless and silly performance, and then Mott declared that he was satisfied.

"Don't have a relapse," he said warningly, and then, turning to Will Phelps, he said, "Now I want my nice little boy, mamma's pet and papa's joy, to show what a good little boy he really is. He isn't going to do any of the naughty things that some of the wicked little college boys do. He is strong, he is, and he promised mamma he wouldn't, and he won't. Let's give him a song, fellows," he added, turning to his classmates, and at once the boys began to sing:

"We're coming, we're coming, our brave little band,On the right side of temperance we always do stand;We don't use tobacco, for this we do think,That those who do use it most always do drink."

Some of the singers had very musical voices and the simple little ditty sounded very clear and strong as they all joined in it. Will Phelps, however, was thinking of what it was that would be required of him. Then flashed into his mind the last conversation he had had with his mother and in which he had given her a promise not unlike that at which Mott had hinted. And he intended to keep it too, he assured himself. Come what might, he would not break it. He even smiled slightly as he thought of what his mother's feelings would be if she could look into Peter John's room and see what was then going on there.

As the song ceased abruptly Will said, "What is it you want me to do, Mott?"

"Well, now, freshman, that's cool. You can't help being a freshman, but it's not well even for a freshman to be too fresh. Ever hear the like of that, fellows?" he inquired of his classmates.

"Never did. Never did," responded several, shaking their heads soberly.

"Just think of it," began Mott again. "Here's a freshman who is so anxious to get into our good graces that he's not only willing to do what we tell him but he even comes and asks us what it is we want him to do. That beats anything old Winthrop has ever seen yet."

Will's face flushed, but he was silent, though Hawley began to laugh again. "Now, then, freshman," said Mott, pointing his finger at Will, "we want you to get down on the floor and wrestle with temptation."

"There's nothing here that tempts me very much," replied Will coolly, and Hawley promptly laughed aloud.

"You do as I tell you! Get down on the floor and wrestle with temptation," demanded Mott sharply.

"I don't mind doing it if it will please you any," responded Will as he slipped from his seat on the table to the floor."That's the way. Now then, papa's joy and mamma's pet, show us how it is that you do the trick."
Stretched upon the floor, Will Phelps went through his struggle with an imaginary foe. He twisted and writhed and struggled, shrieks of laughter

greeting his efforts from the assembled sophomores, and even Hawley joined in, so ridiculous was the appearance which Will presented.
"That's very good, very good indeed!" remarked Mott when several minutes had elapsed. "You'd better get up now and take a seat beside your friend."
Will quickly did as he was bidden, laughing slightly as he glanced at Hawley, whose imperturbable good nature was not in anywise ruffled.
"Hawley, you're a great football player, I understand," said Mott.
"I'm a big player, can't say that I'm great. Some fellows might think so, but it depends on whether they've seen much or know much, I fancy."
"That's right. You're as modest as Mary's little lamb. I hear you're a great sprinter," he added, turning abruptly to Will Phelps.
"Oh, I can run a little. If you'll give me the chance now I'll show you how I can leave the sophs behind," said Will with a laugh, for he was now feeling somewhat the effects of Hawley's manner of meeting his tormentors, and as he glanced down at Peter John it required no deep insight to perceive which was the better way.
The boys in the room laughed good-naturedly and one of them said, "That's enough, Mott. They don't need any more.""Hold on, I'm not done yet," replied Mott. "Tell me what's the name of the little school from which you came," he demanded of Will.
"The Sterling High School."
"And you ran there?"
"A little."
"Get any medals?"
"A few."
"Nice ones! Got any here?"
On his fob Will wore the gold medal he had won the preceding June, but he laughed and made no reply to Mott's question, fearful of incurring further ridicule if he should display the trophy.
"Did you run against the track team of the Meadowbrook Academy?" inquired Mott.
"No. Is that where you fitted?" replied Will simply. Hawley broke into another loud laugh and Mott's face flushed. Will perceived that he had made a mistake and his better plan would be to say as little as possible, whatever the provocation might be or the opening his adversary might give him.
"Did you beat the fast sprinter from the Toad Hollow Institute?" demanded Mott.
"Can't say that I did. I never heard of the school till now."
"Ever run against anybody from the Honeyville Classical Seminary?"
"No."

"Or from the Smartville Four Corners team?"
"We didn't have anything to do with those schools. We weren't in their class."
"Oh, let up, Mott. We've done enough. Let 'em go now," suggested one of the sophomores.
"Not yet," responded Mott. "We must have these freshmen give us an exhibition of what they can do. You fellows take off your collars," he said, turning again to Will and his classmate.
For an instant Will Phelps hesitated and there was a sudden tightening of the muscles in his arms, but Hawley, good-natured and imperturbable as ever, at once removed his collar and Will quietly followed his example.
"That's good," said Mott encouragingly. "Now take out your collar buttons."
Both freshmen obeyed, wondering what was to be required of them. Their curiosity was speedily relieved when Mott said, "We'll have a collar-button race. You two athletes put these buttons on the floor and push them across to the other side of the room with your noses. The one that wins will make the track team here I haven't a doubt."

Hawley again laughed loudly as he and Will took the places assigned them. For a moment their faces were near together and Hawley whispered a few words in Will's ear. His companion's eyes flashed in response, but he did not reply, and in a moment, at Mott's word, the race was begun.

CHAPTER VI

A RACE IN THE DARKNESS

Slowly and steadily the two freshmen began to push the collar buttons across the floor. The floor itself was uncarpeted and not particularly clean, and the position and actions of the two boys certainly did not add to their dignity; but there was not a trace of a smile to be seen on the face of either as they complied with the demands which had been made. The sophomores in the room were also serious, that is, all were save one, and, as he laughed aloud at the ridiculous aspect of their victims, Mott said savagely, "Put him out! He's no business here? Get out of this room!"

The offending sophomore, despite his protests and his promise to "be good," was thrust out from the room, and the race was then resumed. Whenever either of the contestants lagged or one seemed to be gaining slightly upon the other he was sharply bidden to make good his loss, and when the two freshmen had come near the side of the room which they were seeking to gain the collar buttons were close together and each freshman could see the expression on his companion's face. Perhaps it was well for them both that the members of the rival class could not see the quiet glance which Hawley gave Will nor its equally keen response, but the look was understood by both freshmen and they were aware that the critical time in the contest was approaching.

They were by this time within two feet of the door which opened into the hall. The sophomores who had been standing in front of it now moved back to give the contestants room, and as Hawley perceived that the way was clear, after looking up for a moment and glancing keenly at his classmate, he suddenly leaped to his feet and Will instantly followed his example. Before the astonished sophomores were fully aware of what was occurring both had darted through the doorway after Hawley had with almost incredible quickness flung open the door. Instantly it was closed, and Hawley, seizing the iron handle of the catch and putting forth all his strength, braced his feet against the wall and prepared to hold the inmates prisoners in the room.

"Get Andrews and Briggs!" whispered Hawley, and Will quickly darted across the hallway to the room of his two classmates. A word was sufficient to inform them of what was occurring, and in an incredibly brief time all three were standing beside Hawley.

The giant freshman was holding the door, which opened inward, easily, though the sophomores in the room were striving desperately on their side. But Hawley had the strong handle and only the tiny latch could be seized from within. Numbers counted for nothing in this struggle, as only one could pull at a time.

The silence in the building was unbroken, though the first thought of the bold freshmen had been that their sophs would throw open the window and summon their classmates to their aid. Whether it was due to their excitement or to the fact that they did not wish to have their predicament known, Will Phelps never learned, but no outcry was made, though the steady pull upon the door continued.

"I've got 'em!" whispered Hawley gleefully. "If the latch doesn't give way they won't see outdoors again till I give 'em leave. Run, Will!" he added hastily. "Get twenty of our fellows here as soon as you can and we'll fix 'em yet. I can hold on here forever!"

Leaving his classmates at the doorway, Will Phelps ran swiftly down the stairs and sped across the campus to his own room. He found his room-mate seated at his desk, evidently hard at work. Foster glanced up reprovingly as Will burst into the room and said, "I thought, Will, you were—"

He stopped abruptly as he perceived how excited his classmate was, but before he could make any inquiries Will broke in: "We've got a lot of sophs shut up in Peter John's room! Get some of the fellows and make for the room! Hawley's holding 'em in! Tell Jones and Camp to come and then tell them to get some more and every one to bring two or three with him. Get some more yourself and I'll do the same."

Before his astonished room-mate could make any further inquiries, Will darted out of the room and ran down the stairway covering three steps at a leap. But Foster understood what it was that was demanded of him, and, without hesitating an instant, seized his cap and swiftly followed.

The scheme worked marvelously well, and within five minutes a band of twenty-five freshmen had assembled in the hall in front of Peter John's and Hawley's room in Leland. Hawley was still holding the door and no outcry from within the room had been heard.

"How many sophs room in this entry?" said Will quickly.

"Four," replied Hawley. "Two in the front corner room on the second floor and two in the back corner."

"Can you hold on till we can fix them?"

"I can hold on forever. But you'd better be quick about it."

At Will's word four of his classmates followed him to the floor below and two were speedily assigned to hold one door while two more held the other. They were to be quiet, and, if no outbreak was made, then they were not to make their presence known, but under no circumstances were the sophomores to be permitted to come out from their rooms.

As soon as this arrangement had been perfected Will ran swiftly back to join Hawley and his classmates on the floor above. Hawley was still standing at his post of duty, but as Will approached he laughed silently and whispered:

"What'll we do now, fellows?"

Several whispered suggestions were made, but at last it was agreed that the assembled freshmen should step back on either side and that Hawley should permit the door to be partly opened. It was confidently believed that the sophomores would rush out, and, if they did, a half-dozen were to be permitted to come forth and these were to be seized as silently as possible and bound by the freshmen as their own unfortunate classmate, Peter John Schenck, had already been treated. When a few had emerged and been seized then Hawley was to strive to close the door again and hold the others within, and, with the force thus divided, no strong resistance could be made and the treatment which they were to receive could be determined upon.

As soon as this decision had been made Hawley withdrew from the door, but there was no pressure upon it from within, and for a moment the assembled freshmen stared blankly at one another as if they feared that their game had escaped them and that they themselves were the ones to appear in the unenviable light. Will Phelps advanced as if he was about to open the door, but a silent gesture from Hawley caused him to abandon the project. As he stepped back the latch clicked and the door was suddenly opened. Evidently the inmates were surprised that the door was free, and three or four cautiously stepped forth to peer into the dimly lighted hall. Before they were fully aware of the true condition of affairs they were seized by the waiting freshmen. There were sounds of a momentary struggle, but when those who were within the room attempted to come forth the door was quickly closed in their faces and they were prisoners again. The four who had been seized were quickly bound, and then the assembly turned once more to the door itself.

"We'll go in," said Hawley, "and you musn't let a soph get past you. We must hold every one in there. Now then!" he added, as he pushed gently against the door.

But the door failed to yield to the pressure. For a moment the astounded freshmen knew not what to make of the unexpected resistance, and then as a slight sound from within the room could be heard, Hawley grimly braced himself against the door and whispering to his classmates began to exert all his strength in his endeavor to open it.

For a brief time it resisted all their efforts, and then with a resounding crash it suddenly yielded. But it seemed to the startled freshmen as if the very walls themselves were giving way. There were the sound of falling pieces of furniture and in the midst of the confusion several of the sophomores suddenly darted from the room, and before their enemies could recover from their surprise had gained the head of the stairway and were fleeing from the building.

"Take after 'em! Don't let 'em get away!" called Hawley. "Hold on, it's all right," he quickly added as he perceived Mott in the room. "We don't care for anybody else for we've got the ringleader right here. Let 'em go! Let 'em all go! We don't want anybody else."

There was a momentary hesitation on the part of the sophomores as if they were minded to stand by their classmate, but as they peered about them it seemed almost as if the entire freshman class were present, and instantly discretion became the better part of valor, and they fled in a body from the room and also from the building.

Several of the freshmen had seized Mott by this time, and his desperate attempts to free himself were unavailing. Peter John had been quickly freed by Will Phelps, and then Will said hastily to Hawley:

"We've stirred up the hornets' nest enough, haven't we? The sophs will be back here with all their class. Shall we let him go?"

"Let him go?" laughed Hawley, whose enjoyment seemed to be increasing with every passing moment. "Well, I rather think not."

"What shall we do? They'll be back here in a minute."

"Send everybody to his room. We'll look after this fellow ourselves."

Will Phelps turned to his classmates and said: "Get away from this fellows. The sophs will be here in a minute and we may all be hauled up before the faculty. We'll look after Mott."

Instantly the freshmen ran from Leland Hall, leaving Will Phelps and Foster Bennett, and Peter John and his room-mate to look after the captive sophomore.

"What'll we do with him?" inquired Will hastily.

"Take him over to your room."

"That'll be the first place they'll come to when they don't find him here. Still, I'm perfectly willing—"

"Take him out in the grove," suggested Foster quickly. "If we can get away from here without being seen we'll be all right there."

"That's the thing," assented Hawley. "Foster, you run ahead and see if the coast is all clear, for we may have to carry this fellow, and we might attract some attention if we should happen to be seen on the street."

"No, you won't. I'll go along all right," spoke up Mott. "It's your turn now, but it'll be mine again, you know, and I'll see that you freshmen pay up all your scores with good interest!""Don't you threaten us!" said Peter John angrily, speaking now for the first time.

"I'm not threatening you, freshman, I'm just telling you what you'll have to go through, that's all. You can do with me what you please, but whatever you do you musn't forget that it'll be paid back five times over."

"Don't stop here any longer. Come ahead, fellows," said Hawley quickly.

The party with Mott in their midst swiftly passed down the stairway and turned into the street that led toward "the grove," a clump of huge pine trees that had stood for many years on the borders of the rear campus of the college. The freshmen glanced anxiously about them, but apparently their presence was not noted by the few who were to be seen on the street, and they quickly increased the pace at which they were moving.

As they turned into the campus, Mott suddenly broke away from his captors who had been somewhat deceived by the apparent willingness with which he had followed them, and began to run swiftly back toward the college buildings. The sophomore was known as one of the fleetest footed men in college, and already Will Phelps had had him pointed out as one of the few who had "made" the track team in his freshman year. He had looked up to him with the respect that only a freshman can know for the prominent men in college life, and now was his opportunity to test his own ability against that of the fleeing member of the sophomore class.Quickly he darted in pursuit, feeling rather than perceiving that his own classmates were speedily left far behind him. He was exerting himself to the utmost and ran as though the prize he was seeking was the greatest of coveted honors. As he sped over the grass his respect for his rival increased greatly, for whatever Mott's defects might be, there certainly was in him no lack of ability to run. The distance between the runners was steadily maintained, and indeed, it seemed to Will as if it was being increased. On and on he ran, and the college buildings were now near-by, and if the fleeing sophomore should once gain an entrance in one of them then Will knew all further pursuit would be useless.

Suddenly the form of Mott disappeared in the dim light and Will Phelps stopped abruptly and peered keenly before him. But when his classmates joined him and all four cautiously advanced, several minutes elapsed before a solution for the mystery was found.

CHAPTER VII

SPLINTER'S QUESTIONS

Directly before them the boys could see a long ditch or trench which had been dug the entire length of the back campus and of whose existence they had not been aware. Doubtless Mott had known of it, however, and in his flight had made for it with all the speed he could command, either hoping to lead his pursuers into difficulty or trusting that it in some way would provide a means of escape for himself.

Whatever his plan may have been it succeeded admirably, for when the four freshmen stood together on the border of the trench not a sign of the presence of Mott could be discovered. In which direction he had fled they were also ignorant. It was evident however that he was gone and after a careful search had confirmed the conviction in their minds that the sophomore had escaped, Will Phelps said:

"We'll have to give it up, fellows. He's gone."

"We can go up to his room and get him," suggested Peter John, who was becoming exceedingly bold under the confidence which the presence of his friends gave him.

"We can, but we won't," said Hawley bluntly.

"Why not?" demanded Schenck.

"It's one thing to defend yourself, but it's another to fly straight into the arms of the sophs. I don't wonder that some of the freshmen get into trouble, they're so fresh. If the sophs didn't take it out of them I think our own class itself would."

"That's so," responded Peter John cordially, "I've thought of it myself lots of times. Now there's Merrivale—he rooms next to me, you know—he ought to be shown that he's too fresh."

"What's he done?" inquired Foster.

"Why he came into my room last week and borrowed fifty cents, and he hasn't paid it back yet, either!"

"Oh, well, just remember what Mott said, Peter John."

"What did he say?"

"He said every freshman would be paid back with interest."

"I don't want any interest," declared Peter John in all seriousness. "I'll be satisfied if I'm paid back without that."

"You'll get it, though," laughed Will; and as his two companions also joined in his laugh Peter John said no more, except that he "couldn't see anything very funny in that."

The boys, however, did not longer delay where they were but quietly returned to their rooms, nor were they again disturbed that night. Indeed, for several days the quiet of the college life was not ruffled and both Will Phelps and his room-mate began to hope that their troubles were at an end. Mott, whom they saw on the following morning when they were departing from chapel, laughed good-naturedly as he greeted them and indeed his friendship for them seemed to be increased by the recent experiences through which he had passed. Several times he came to the room of Will and Foster and remained until his welcome was decidedly that was displeasing to both the boys, though there threadbare. There was something in his bearing was a certain indefinable something about him that was not altogether unpleasant. His language, his bearing, and his general appearance all betokened a certain coarseness of fibre that somehow grated upon the feelings of Will and his room-mate, though they could not have explained even to themselves just what it was. He was such a marked man in college, however, and was looked up to by so many that there was a certain pleasure in his personal attention and both Will and Foster felt in a measure the flattery of his evident favor.

The college work had now begun to settle into its regular grooves and when another week had elapsed, Will and Foster began to feel that the spirit of their surroundings had to an extent been received by them and that they were indeed a part of the life. There were moments now that came to Will, when do what he might he could not banish from his mind the thought of the home in Sterling of which practically he was no longer a part. The vision of his father seated in his easy-chair in the library of an evening, before the fire that glowed upon the hearth, his paper in his hands and the very manner in which he occasionally glanced up and read to his mother something he had noticed seemed to be one that Will could not shake off. The pictures on the walls, the very rugs on the floor, and the chairs in the room could all be distinctly seen, and somehow the sight never failed to bring a certain depression with it. Will

Phelps would indignantly have denied that he was homesick, but as the days came and went his manner became somewhat subdued and when he rose from his bed in the early morning and peered forth from his bedroom window at the towering hills that were all aglow with the glory of the rising sun, somehow their very beauty and grandeur seemed to deepen his feeling that he was "a good way off," as he expressed it, though just what it was that was so far away he could only have vaguely expressed or defined. Doubtless his room-mate could have explained to him that it was the little city of Sterling that now seemed to be so remote, for he too was suffering slightly from the same malady that troubled his friend.

Why is it that most boys are so afraid to acknowledge that they are ever homesick? Is it the fear that they may appear too dependent and less manly if they confess their longing for home? Certainly no boy who comes from a good home detracts from his own strength of character by acknowledging that he misses the home from which he has gone. Indeed, is it not a reflection upon the boy and the home alike, if he declares when he goes from his father's house that he misses nothing? To yield to the feeling of homesickness, to permit it to overmaster one and prevent him from performing his tasks in the place wherein he finds himself may be a confession of weakness, but to suffer nothing from it is to declare a weakness or defect greater still. And Will Phelps, though he was silent as to his own feelings, was suffering keenly in the early days of his life in Winthrop.

A week had elapsed since the events recorded in the preceding chapter and Will and Foster were studying busily in their rooms one evening, striving to hold their wearied minds to their work, for there had been an unexpected written test that day in their Greek and both were somewhat anxious as to the results of their efforts.

Suddenly the door opened and in walked Peter John, who had already acquired the collegiate habit of never inquiring if his presence was welcome in the room into which he came. His face was beaming and it was at once evident to both Will and Foster that their classmate had something of importance to declare.

"How'd you get along in the test to-day, fellows?" was Peter John's first question.

"Not very well," replied Will, motioning for his visitor to be seated.

"I just killed it."

Will and Foster laughed as they heard Peter John already indulging in college slang. It seemed so out of keeping with his general bearing and appearance. The gap between his trousers and his shoes had never been so apparent, his splotches so vivid, nor his hair so belligerent as now.

"There's that question, 'Who were the mercenaries of the Greeks, and what was a mercenary?' I got that right, I know I did."

"How did you answer it?" inquired Foster.

"Why, I said 'a mercenary was a man that sold himself to some one,' and I showed what I meant by illustrating it."

"How?"

"I said the professors were the mercenaries of the college."

"You did?" exclaimed Will, sitting instantly erect.

"Yes, sir; I did. What's the matter?" he added, as both boys began to laugh loudly. "Isn't it true?"

"Oh, it's too good to be true. Tell us some more, Peter John."

"I can't see what you fellows are laughing at," said Peter John soberly. "That answered the question all right. I'll get an 'A' on that paper. Then there was that question, 'What was the Greek law and conception of vengeance?' That bothered me a bit at first, but I got it, I'm sure."

"What did you say?" inquired Will.

"Why, that's as plain as the nose on your face," responded Peter John glibly. "I said that vengeance was a low-down, mean, spiteful attempt to pay back. 'Vengeance is mine and I will repay,' saith the Lord."

"Oh, you'll get more than 'A' on that," said Will in the extremity of his delight, as he was compelled to go to the window and gaze out into the night. "You'll get at least A square."

"No, I won't. They don't give that. 'A' is the highest mark they give. But I think I got everything right. How did you answer that question about what Christian tenet the Greeks believed in?" he added, glancing at the copy of the questions which he held in his hands.

"How did you answer it, Peter John?" inquired Foster quickly.

"I answered it that they believed in the immorality of the soul."

"In the what?" demanded Foster soberly.
"In the immorality of the soul."
"You meant immortality of the soul, didn't you?"
"Y-e-s, I suppose I did," assented Peter John somewhat ruefully. "But old Splinter will understand," he added quickly. "Splinter will know I just left out a 't', and he won't count that against me."
"No, a little thing like a 't' doesn't count for much, not any more than a decimal point. It doesn't make any difference whether a decimal point is placed before or after a figure, you know. It's only a little thing anyway."
"Yes," assented Peter John, failing to perceive what Foster was saying. "Then there was one other question that was dead easy," he added.
"Which one was that?"
"The one about the animals."
"Let me see, what was that question?" said Foster thoughtfully.
"Why, don't you remember? It was 'Name six animals that were common among the Greeks'."
"Oh, yes; I recall it now; but I don't think I had it right. I could think of but four."
"Pooh! Easiest question of the whole lot."
"What was the answer?"
"Easy! Dead easy! I just said, 'Six dogs'."
The laughter that rang out in the room might have been heard across the campus; but Peter John was only slightly ruffled, and said:
"Oh, well, you fellows may laugh if you want to, but you'll find out when you see my marks."
"They'll put you in Splinter's place as soon as you graduate," suggested Foster when at last he regained control of himself.
"I wish they would," responded Will heartily.
"Splinter" was the term by which the Winthrop boys were accustomed to speak of Professor Hanson, who was in charge of their Greek work. The title did not appear in the college catalog, it was true; but it was the only one by which he was known among the irreverent students. He was an elderly man, whose sensitive nature had suffered for many years from the inadequate preparation of successive classes, until at last not only were his teeth on edge, but his entire disposition as well. He had become somewhat soured and sarcastic in his dealings with the students, and was more unpopular than any other

professor in the college. His scholarship was accurate. His ability to impart his knowledge to such students as were eager to learn was also unquestioned, but for the indifferent and lazy, or for the dull or poorly prepared, his words were like drops of vitriol.
His popular title of Splinter had been bestowed upon him because of certain physical characteristics however. He was a very tall man and exceedingly thin, and the very beard which he wore imparted by its sharp point an additionally suggestive emphasis to his slight and slender frame. No one knew how the title originated or how it came to be bestowed upon the professor; but its appropriateness had at once fastened the term and every entering class received it as a heritage from those which had preceded it.
Will Phelps already had acquired a keen dislike for the man, and he had laughed heartily when Mott one night had declared that the student body had been compelled to give Professor Hanson the new name he had received. "You see," Mott had said, "the faculty and the trustees decide what titles a man can wear after his name; so it's only fair that the students should decide what titles he shall wear beforehis name. Now this man's name used to be simply John Hanson. Then some college or other said it should be John Hanson, PH.D. Well, the students here have only gone a step further and they've not taken anything away from the old fellow. They've added to him, that's what they have; and now it's Prof. Splinter John Hanson, PH.D. He ought to be grateful, but it's a cold world and I sometimes fear he doesn't appreciate what was done for him. In fact such bestowments are rarely received as they should be."

The suggestion Will's room-mate had made that Peter John soon might take Splinter's place had recalled his own difficulties with the man, but soon even the thoughts of the unpopular professor of Greek were forgotten in the new interest that was aroused by the entrance into the room of three young men who were at once recognized as members of the junior class.

CHAPTER VIII

THE PARADE

"You're just the fellows we're looking for," said Allen, the leading spirit of the three young men who entered the room.

"You haven't very far to look, then," replied Will laughingly, for in his heart he felt honored by the unexpected visit of the upper classmen.

"That's right, freshman. How are you getting on?"

"They've kept us busy, to say the least."

"You mean the sophs?"

"Yes. That's the only class we have to think of, isn't it?"

"No. Your own class is first."

"It's the best class in college," interrupted Peter John quickly, and all who were in the room laughed as the uncouth freshman's face flushed.

"That's the way to talk," responded Allen.

"But it is. I'm not joking," persisted Peter John seriously.

"No doubt. No doubt. But what we've come for is to tell you about the parade."

"Parade? What parade?" inquired Foster.

"Why, every fall there is a parade of the freshmen. They have a band usually, at least most of the classes have had one and as yours is the best class that ever entered college, why you won't want to fall behind the others I know."

"Who pays for the band?" demanded Peter John.

"You do, that is, your class does."

"I won't pay a cent," retorted Peter John.

"You don't have to," laughed Allen. "Some of the others will make it up. I'm just telling you what the custom is and only for your own good."

"Go on with your story," interrupted Will. "Let's hear about the parade."

"It's to come off next Saturday afternoon, and we juniors usually help out in the scheme, you see. We try to arrange a part of it for you and help you out in some of the details. The whole thing is 'horse play,' just a sort of burlesque, and the more ridiculous you can make it, the better."

"I'll not make a fool of myself for anybody," spoke up Peter John sharply.

"You don't have to. It won't be necessary," replied Allen quietly, but in the laugh that followed, Peter John took no part.

"What do you want us to do?" inquired Foster.

"Well, we suggest that this young man—I've forgotten his name," said Allen, turning to Peter John as he spoke.

"Schenck. Peter John Schenck—that's my name, and I'm not ashamed of it either!" said that worthy promptly. "But I don't propose to hire a band and march around the streets making a fool of myself for anybody."

"You don't have to," and again a laugh arose at the junior's words. "I was only suggesting, that's all. But if you want to know what I think, I'm of the opinion that if you'd be one to help haul the committee from the senior class around in their chariot it would be a good thing for you. That's only a suggestion on my part, as I told you, and you can do as you please about it."

"I don't please to do it," replied Peter John sulkily.

"What's the 'chariot' you spoke of, Allen?" inquired Will.

"Oh, it's only an old hay wagon. It's been the custom for some of the freshmen to haul the officers of the senior class around in it. It doesn't amount to much, but honestly I think it will be a good thing for you to do it."

"All right, you can count on me," said Will quickly.

"I don't want to count on that from you. I've something else for you and Bennett to do."

"What's that?"

"I'll explain it to you." And Allen at once went into the details of the scheme he proposed. Both Will and Foster laughed as he laid it before them, and willingly consented to do their part. Peter John, however, said not a word, and when the visitors prepared to depart, Allen said, "You're to assemble at the gym, you know, and the parade will be formed in front of it on the street. It'll march up Main Street, down East End Avenue, around through Walker Street, up West Street, across Drury Lane and then back into Main Street and then on down to the ball ground. There the parade will break up and the freshmen and sophomores will have their annual ball game. It'll be great fun if you take it in the right spirit, and you'll have plenty of spectators too."

"How's that?" said Foster.

"Why, the whole college, faculty and all, will turn out to see it, and of course all the village people will be on hand, and if it's a good day there'll be a crowd here from out of town. The trains will be crowded that day, and there'll be a good many who'll come into Winthrop with their automobiles. You'll never forget the day as long as you live."

"Great!" exclaimed Will. "I wish it was to-morrow. Where shall we get these things we're to wear?"

"You can find them in the stores, or maybe I'll be able to help you out some. Come down to my room to-morrow and I'll see what can be done. Good night," Allen added, as he and his classmates started down the stairway.

"Good night," responded Will and Foster, and then closed the door.

"Of all the foolishness I ever heard that beats all," said Peter John when the freshmen were by themselves once more. "They don't get me into it."

"Oh, yes, Peter John. Don't pull off that way," said Will cordially.

"Not much. I'm not so big a fool as they take me to be."

"You'll be a bigger one if you keep out."

"Maybe I will, but I'm not going to go into any such doings."

"Now look here, Peter John. You're a freshman, but you can't help that and no one blames you for it. I'm—"

"I'm no more a freshman than you are," retorted Peter John warmly.

"Right you are. But you don't want to make a bad matter worse. If you keep out you'll be a marked man and everybody in college will hear about it. It'll be a great deal better for you to go in quietly, and whatever you think about it, just keep your thoughts to yourself, and don't call the attention of the whole college to you by your foolishness. It'll be simply a challenge for the sophs, if you don't do it, and you'll be the one to suffer."

"You think so?"

"I know so."

"I guess the sophs found out what sort of a fellow I was the other night. I'd have brained the first one that laid hands on me."

"You didn't though, and you wouldn't. It's a great deal better to do as Hawley did and just laugh it off."

"Oh, I laughed all right, and I'd have given those fellows something to laugh about too, if they hadn't tied me up."

"Of course, but the trouble is they did tie you up, and the next time it'll be worse than that. It isn't worth while to kick too hard, Peter John. A fellow has just got to take some things in life as he finds them and not as he'd like to have them. It's the only way, and the sooner he learns it the better."

"But my father told me never to let anybody impose on me," said Peter John dubiously.

"Nobody is going to impose on you. You won't be doing anything more than every fellow in the class, and if you don't go in you'll be the one marked exception. The sophs will take it as an invitation."

"You think so, do you?"

"Yes, sir, I do. Come along, Peter John, and don't make any more fuss about it.""Well, I'll think about it," replied the freshman as he departed for his own room in Leland Hall.

Saturday dawned bright and clear and the interest and excitement in the college over the parade rose to its highest point. A band had been secured from a neighboring city, and in the afternoon, when its stirring strains were heard from the steps of the gymnasium, all the freshmen were made aware that the time for their assembly had arrived. There were crowds of strangers to be seen about the streets and the little town was all active with unwonted bustle.

Automobiles were arriving, the sophomores were assembling at the various buildings, and their jeers and cries could be heard as they greeted the appearance of the members of the class below them when they started for the gymnasium.

Will Phelps and Foster Bennett felt keenly the prevailing excitement, and when they entered the gymnasium building they found a large number of their own classmates already assembled and keenly alive to the demands that were soon to be made upon them.

Under the experienced guidance of the committee of juniors the freshmen were soon equipped for their various parts and the procession was formed. In advance moved the band and behind it was a huge hay wagon in which in great dignity were seated six of the seniors. The wagon itself was drawn by sixteen freshmen, all of whom had a tight grasp upon the ropes that had been fastened to the wagon tongue. Directly behind the wagon came Will Phelps and Foster Bennett and two of their classmates, all dressed in the garb of firemen, with red jackets and helmet hats of paper. In their hands was a huge rope at least two and a half inches in diameter, which was attached to a tiny tin fire engine not more than a foot in length. Behind the firemen came Hawley, who was dressed as an infant with a lace cap on his head and carefully tied bows under his chin, while in his hands he was carrying a bottle of milk. He was seated in an improvised baby carriage, which was being pushed by one of the smallest members of the freshman class. "Sunny Jim," Charley Chaplin and Ben Turpin were among the characters that could be seen in the long lines of freshmen that, three abreast, were arranged still farther back in the procession, and at last, at the word of Allen, the junior who was acting as the marshal of the day, the march was begun. Frequently Will turned and glanced behind him at the long, tortuous line, and its ridiculous appearance caused him to laugh and say to Foster:

"Did you ever see anything in your life like that?"

"I never did."

"Silence there in the ranks!" called Allen sharply, for he chanced to be marching near the "fire engine." Not a trace of a smile could be seen on his face, and to all appearances he was engaged in what he considered one of the most serious events of his life.

In the streets the people were lined up and their laughter and good-natured applause could be heard on every side. Small boys followed the line of march or walked beside the long column, and their derisive remarks were frequent and loud. The sophomores also added their comments, but there was no open disturbance throughout the march. It was one of the events of freshman year and as such was evidently not to be entered upon lightly or unadvisedly, like certain other important epochs in life.

At last the procession arrived at the athletic field and there broke up for the baseball game with the sophomores. The grand stand was already filled with the people and students that had watched the march, and, as soon as Will and Foster had donned their baseball suits, for both had been selected to play on the freshman nine, they appeared upon the field, where already the other members of the team were awaiting their coming.

"I didn't see Peter John, did you, Foster?" inquired Will.

"No. It'll be all the worse for him, I fancy."

"No doubt about that. What are we going to do with him, Foster?"

"Nothing."

"I don't like to see the chap suffer for his own foolishness."

"Neither do I. But he'll have to learn for himself. You can't tell him anything."

"You can tell him all right enough, but I'm afraid that's all the good it does. You might as well try to polish sponge."

The conversation ceased as the call for the game to be begun was heard and both boys hastened to take the positions in which they were to play. The noise among the spectators increased as the signal was given, but for three innings both nines played earnestly and seriously. At the end of the third inning, with the score standing five to four in favor of the sophomores, a radical change was made. The batter was blindfolded and compelled to stand upon an upturned barrel, which was substituted for the home plate. The pitcher and catcher were each also to stand upon a barrel and the pitcher was ordered to throw the ball with his left hand. Naturally it was impossible for the batter to hit the ball, since he was blindfolded, and when three strikes had been called he tore the bandage from his eyes and upon his hands and knees was compelled to crawl toward first base. The baseman stood with his back to the field and naturally found it difficult to secure the ball which had been thrown by the left hand of the catcher. Shrieks of laughter arose from the spectators, shouts and class cries were heard on every side, tin horns mingled their noise with the blasts of the band, and altogether Will Phelps thought that the scene was unique in the experiences of his young life.

CHAPTER IX

THE WALK WITH MOTT

In the days that immediately followed the freshman parade and the burlesque game of baseball with the rival class, the work before Will Phelps and his room-mate settled more deeply into its regular grooves. The novelty of the new life was now gone and to Will it almost seemed that ages had passed since he had been a member of the household in Sterling. His vision of the hilltops from his bedroom window became longer and he could see in his mind far behind the towering barriers of the hills into the familiar street and well-remembered rooms of his father's house. The foliage on the hillsides now had assumed its gorgeous autumn dress and wherever he looked the forests seemed to be clad as if they were all on dress parade. The sight was beautiful and one which in after years was ever present with him; but in those early days of his freshman year in Winthrop, it seemed somehow to impress him as a great barrier between his home and the place where he then was.

However, he never referred to his feeling to any one, not even to Foster, and strove manfully to bear it all. He was working well, but in his Greek he was finding increasing difficulty. This he acknowledged in part was due to his own neglect in the earlier years of his preparatory course, but boy-like he attributed most of his lack of success in that department to "Splinter," for whom he came to cherish a steadily increasing dislike. The man's personality was exceedingly irritating to the young freshman and his dislike for the professor was becoming intense—a marked contrast to his feeling for his teacher in mathematics for whom he entertained a regard that was but little short of adoration. His knowledge evidently was so great, and his inspiring personality in the classroom was so enjoyable that Will soon found himself working in that department as he never before had worked in his brief life. Already, the boys were referring to him as a "shark," and the praise of his classmates was sweet. But in Greek—that was an altogether different affair, he declared. Splinter was so cold-blooded, so unsympathetic, and sarcastic, he appeared to be so fond of "letting a fellow make a fool of himself in recitation," as Will expressed it, that he found but little pleasure in his work. And Will had already suffered from the keen shafts of the teacher's merciless ridicule. One day, when in fact he had spent an additional hour in the preparation of his lesson in Greek, though the results he had achieved left him still troubled as he thought of the recitation, he had been called upon to translate and make comments upon a portion of the lesson of the day. He could feel as well as see, or at least he fancied that he saw, the drawing down of Splinter's lips that presaged an outburst of sarcasm. Will had been permitted to go through his task without interruption and then the professor had said dryly, "That will do, Mr. Phelps. That is what one might term 'making Greek' of it. It certainly is justice neither to the Greek nor to the English." A partly suppressed titter had run through the class at the biting words, and with face flushed scarlet Will Phelps had resumed his seat, feeling that in all the world there could not be found another man so thoroughly despicable as Splinter. And his feeling of dislike had increased with the passing days. He had come not only to detest the man, but the Greek as well. If he could have followed his own desire he would have abandoned the subject at once and substituted something in its place, but Will understood fully his father's desire for him to become proficient in that department and how useless it would be for him to write home for the desired permission. In sheer desperation he began to devote additional time to his study of Greek, until he felt that he was almost neglecting certain other studies in his course that in themselves were far more enjoyable. But his progress under Splinter seemed to be in no wise advanced, and soon Will was cherishing a feeling that was something between a hopeless rage and an ungovernable detestation.

One break had occurred, however, in that both he and Foster had joined one of the Greek letter fraternities—the Phi Alpha. Both freshmen were now taking their meals at the fraternity house and in the good fellowship and the presence of his fellow-members he found a measure of relief from the homesickness that was troubling him and his difficulties with the detested professor of Greek. It was also a source of some comfort to him to learn that his own feeling for Splinter was one that was commonly held by all the students who had been under him; but though his misery may have loved the company, his problem still remained his own and appeared to be as far from solution as ever.

Not long after Will and Foster had joined the Phi Alpha fraternity, Peter John had dropped into their room one evening and quickly discovered the neat little badge or pin that each boy wore on his vest directly over his heart.

"Hello!" exclaimed Peter John; "you've joined the Phi Alpha, have you?"

"Yes," replied Will quietly, striving then to change the topic of conversation, for the subject was one not to be cheapened by ordinary remarks.

"It's about the best in college, isn't it?" persisted Peter John.

"That's not for us to say," laughed Will.

"I haven't joined any fraternity yet," said Peter John. "My father told me I'd better wait and perhaps he'd come up to Winthrop a little later and then he'd tell me which one to join."

Will and Foster glanced at each other, but neither spoke. In fact there was nothing to say.

"If you feel sure the Phi Alpha's the best, I might write home to my father and perhaps he'd let me join now," suggested Peter John. "He thinks that whatever you two fellows do is about right."

As only about half the students in Winthrop were members of the Greek letter fraternities, and as those who were elected were chosen because of certain elements in their characters or lives that made them specially desirable as companions or comrades, the election was naturally looked upon as an especial honor and many of the entering class had been eagerly awaiting the invitation for which all longed. Peter John Schenck's unique personality and his sublime self-assurance had been qualities, if no other defects had been apparent, that would have debarred him, but he was so sublimely unconscious of all this—"Not even knowing enough to know that he didn't know, the worst form of ignorance in all the world," Foster had half angrily declared—that not for a moment did he dream that his membership was something perhaps undesirable of itself.

"I might write home and ask him," suggested Peter John when neither of his classmates responded. "I think I like the Phi Alpha pretty well myself."

"I wouldn't do it," said Foster. "How are you making out with Splinter?" he added, striving to change the subject.

"Oh, Splinter's all right."

"Glad you think so," said Will bitterly.

"Some of the fellows think he's hard, but he's all right if you know how to handle him," declared Peter John pompously. "I'll put down a good mark for him."

"Good for you, Peter John!" laughed Foster. "Wait till he puts down your mark."

"I'll get an 'A' in Greek."

"I hope you'll give me a part of it then," said Will. "Did you ever see such a fellow?" he said to Foster when their visitor had departed.

"I never did. I don't mind him myself, but for his own sake I wish he could learn something. I don't believe he'll ever do it though."

"I'm afraid he'll be taught some things that are not in the course of study.""Do him good," remarked Foster, as he turned once more to his work.

The following day was Saturday, and in the afternoon there were no recitations. Will had promised Mott that he would go for a long walk with him, and promptly after luncheon the sophomore appeared. For some reason which Will could not explain, Mott appeared to have taken a decided fancy to him, and had paid him many special attentions. There was little about him that was attractive to Will, but somehow he found it difficult to avoid him. He certainly was a well dressed handsome young fellow, and was prominent in college chiefly because of his success in athletics, for already he had the reputation of being one of the swiftest runners in college. But in the college vernacular he was commonly referred to as a "sport," a term for which Will instinctively had little liking, and less for the young man himself. However, he had found it difficult to avoid him, and somewhat reluctantly he had consented to take the long walk to a distant village with him on the day to which reference has been made.

For a time after the two young men had departed from Winthrop, and had made their way up the road that led along the steep hillside, the exhilaration of the bracing air and the superb view had made Will keenly alive to the beauties of the surrounding region. A soft halo covered the summits of the lofty hills, and the quiet of the valley was almost as impressive as the framework of the mountains. Mott too had been exceedingly pleasant in all that he had said, and Will was almost beginning to feel that he had misjudged his companion, and that his reputation was worse than the fellow himself.

They had now left the hillside road and were once more in the valley and not far from the village they were seeking.

"I hear you're quite a fair sprinter," suggested Mott, as they proceeded.

"I do a little," assented Will, laughing lightly as he spoke.

"Where did you run?"

"On the high school team."

"What high school?"

"Sterling."

"Run against the other schools in the league?"

"Yes," replied Will, wondering how it was that Mott happened to know of the existence of the league.

"How did you come out?"

"Oh, I happened to win. There wasn't very much to run against, you see."

"What time did you make?"

"Ten, two."

"Going to run here?"

"Going to try to."

"I find this taking long walks is good for me," said Mott. "It keeps my muscles in trim and gives me wind."

This, then, was the object which Mott had in view in inviting him to take the walk, Will hastily concluded. He wanted to find out all he could learn about his ability as a runner, and in spite of himself Will was flattered by the evident interest and attention. They were now within the confines of the village, and excusing himself for a moment Mott left Will, but when he returned it was evident from the odor about him that the sophomore had been to some speakeasy. Will had known of Mott's habits, and the fact that he had left him and gone alone to secure his drink argued that the fellow was not altogether bad.

There was not a long delay in the village, and the return by a different road from that by which they had come was suggested by Mott, and Will had acquiesced. They had not gone far, however, before Mott discovered a farmer approaching with a team and a heavy but empty farm wagon, and quickly suggested that they should ride, and as Will at once agreed, his companion hailed the passing man.

"Hi, grandpa! Will you give us a ride?" he called.

Without a word the farmer, who was an old man, halted his team and permitted the boys to clamber up into the wagon.

"This is more like it," said Mott, forgetful of the benefits of walking, as the horses started.

"It's not half bad," replied Will, as he glanced at the old man who was driving. A straw hat covered his gray head, and his untrimmed gray beard as well as his somewhat rough clothing could not entirely detract from the keen twinkle in his eyes.

"I fancy," said Mott, addressing the driver, "that the beauties of this country have added much to your longevity?"

"My which?" demanded the farmer sharply.

"Your longevity."

"I never had no such complaint's that. I've had the rheumatiz, but that's all that ever bothered me any."

"You are to be congratulated," murmured Mott.

"Guess that's so. See that buryin' ground over there?" inquired the driver, pointing as he spoke to a quaint little cemetery by the roadside.

"Yes," replied Mott. "Probably most of the people died of longevity."

"It don't tell on th' gravestones. Jest got a new gravedigger."

"How's that?"

"Third we've had inside o' a year. Had one fur nigh onto forty year, but he up an' died."

"Longevity?" gravely inquired Mott.

"Like enough; though some folks thought 'twas softenin' o' th' brain; but my 'pinion is he never had any brains to get soft. Still he were a good digger, but the man we got next was no good."

"What was the trouble with him? More longevity?"

"No; he buried everybody with their feet to the west."

"Isn't that the proper thing?"

"No, 'tisn't!"

"Why?"

"Any fool knows ye ought t' be buried with yer feet t' the east."

"Why's that?"

"So't ye can hear Gabriel's trumpet better when he blows, an' can rise up facin' him an' be all ready t' go when he calls."

"I hadn't thought of that.""Like 's not. Some folks don't. We've got another digger now, an' he knows."

For a time conversation ceased, and the farmer drove briskly along the country road. When an hour had elapsed, Mott said, "I don't see that we're getting anywhere near Winthrop."

"Winthrop? Is that where ye want t' go? Students there, maybe?"

"Yes."

"Well, we've been goin' straight away from Winthrop all the time. Ye didn't say nothin' 'bout it, an' I didn't feel called upon t' explain, for I supposed college students knew everything."

"How far is it to Winthrop?" inquired Will blankly.

"'Beout ten mile," responded the farmer, his eyes twinkling as he reined in his team.

CHAPTER X

A VISITOR

The boys both hastily leaped to the ground and the old farmer quickly spoke to his team and started on, leaving his recent passengers in such a frame of mind that they even forgot to thank him for his courtesy and kindness. As the wagon drove off, Will fancied that he heard a sly chuckle from the driver but he had disappeared around the bend in the road before the young freshman recovered from his astonishment sufficiently to speak of it.

"That old chap wasn't such a fool after all," said Mott glumly.

"That's what he wasn't," responded Will beginning to laugh.

"What are you laughing at?" demanded Mott sharply.

"At ourselves."

"I don't see the joke."

"Might as well laugh as cry."

"You'll sing another song before you're back in Winthrop to-night. Ten miles isn't any laughing matter after we've tramped as far as we have to-day."

"But it'll help us for our track meet," suggested Will, laughing again.

"Bother the track meet!"

"It'll help our longevity then. I've always heard that walking was the best exercise."

"The old fellow was foxy. He never said a word but just let us talk on. I'd give a dollar to hear his account of it when he gets home."

"Cheap enough. But say, Mott, have we got to tramp all the way back to Winthrop?"

"Looks that way."

"Can't we get a car here somewhere?"

"Hardly. We might try it at that farmhouse over yonder," replied Mott pointing toward a low house not far away as he spoke.

"Come ahead! Let's try it anyway," suggested Will eagerly.

The boys at once hastened to the place, and after a brief delay succeeded in summoning the young farmer who lived there. They made their wishes known, but in response the man said, "Can't do it anyhow. My wife's sick and I'm goin' for the doctor now."

"Where is he?" demanded Will eagerly.

"Over at the Junction."

Will knew where the Junction was, a little hamlet about seven miles from Winthrop. How far it was distant from the place where he then was, however, he had no idea. It was easy to ascertain, and in response to his question the farmer explained that it was "about three mile."

"You might take us there, then," said Will quickly. "I don't know just how the trains run for Winthrop, but it'll be three miles nearer anyway."

"Yes, I'll be glad to take you there."

"How much are you going to charge us?" demanded Mott who did not plan to be caught again by the "guilelessness" of any of the people of the region."Oh, I sha'n't charge ye anything. Glad t' do ye the favor," responded the farmer heartily.

In a brief time his car was ready, and, acting upon his suggestion, the boys at once took their places on the seat, and the driver soon was briskly speeding down the roadway.

Conversation lagged, for the boys were somewhat wearied by their long tramp and the young farmer was silent, doubtless anxious over the illness in his home. When a brief time had elapsed he deposited the boys on the platform of the little station at the Junction, and again declining any offer on their part to pay for the service he had rendered them at once departed in his search for the physician.

Approaching the little window in the ticket office Mott inquired, "What's the next train we can get for Winthrop?"

"No more trains to-night," responded the man without looking up from the noisy clicker over which he was bending.

"No more trains?"

"That's what I said. The last one passed here fifteen minutes ago."

"Isn't there any way we can get there?"

"I s'pose there is."

"What is it?" demanded Mott eagerly.

"Walk."

"How far is it?"

"Seven miles."

"And there's no other way?"

"You won't be the first that have counted the ties between Junction and Winthrop.""Isn't there a freight train that comes along pretty soon?" inquired Will.

"There's one that's due in 'bout an hour. But you never can depend on it. It may be here in an hour and it may be three hours. You never can tell."

"What shall we do, Phelps?" inquired Mott, turning sharply to his companion.

"I don't care much, but I believe it would be better for us to start. It isn't so very far and besides it'll be good for our longevity and help us for the meet."

There was an exclamation of anger from Mott who doubtless had become somewhat sensitive to the frequent references to his favorite expression of the day, but he made no protest and the two boys at once started up the track. Both were hungry and weary but the distance must be traversed, and there was no time or breath to waste in complaining. Steadily they trudged onward, the monotony of the walk increased by the deepening darkness. They had been gone from the station only about an hour when the shrill screech of the whistle from a locomotive approaching from behind them was heard, and in a few minutes the long and noisy freight train thundered past them.

Mott was almost beside himself with rage as he watched the passing cars and heaped all manner of maledictions upon the head of the station agent, who, he declared, must have known the train was coming, and with malice aforethought had withheld his knowledge and advised the boys to walk. "Everybody was against the college boys," he declared, "and looked upon it as legitimate to take advantage ofthem in every possible manner." But Will only laughed in response and made no protests though he was as thoroughly wearied as his companion.

At last the lights of the college could be seen and shortly after ten o'clock they arrived at their dormitory. "We'll remember this walk, I take it," said Mott glumly as he turned toward his room.

"We certainly shall," replied Will. "The 'longevity' of that old farmer was something wonderful."

"Bother his longevity!" exclaimed Mott as he turned quickly away.

Left to himself Will slowly climbed the stairs until he arrived at his own room, but as he was about to enter he suddenly stopped and listened intently to the sound of voices within. Surely he knew that voice, he thought, and in an instant opened the door and burst into the room.

Seated in the easy-chair was his father. Instantly Will's weariness was forgotten and with a shout he rushed upon his visitor throwing his arm about his neck and laughing in a way that may have served to keep down a stronger emotion.

"How long have you been here?" he demanded. "Where's mother? When did you come? How's everybody at home? Anything wrong? My, but I'm glad to see you! How long are you going to stay?"

The questions and exclamations fell from Will's lips in such confusion that it was impossible to reply and even Foster who was in the room joined in the laugh with which his room-mate's excitement was greeted."Not too fast, Will," laughed his father. "I had to come near here on business and I thought it would be a good thing to stop at Winthrop over night and have a little visit with my boy. I didn't know that I should be able to have one," he added smilingly, "for he wasn't anywhere to be found."

"I'm sorry! I wish I'd known it. I've been out for a walk with Mott. And we certainly have had one!" he added as he recounted some of the experiences of the afternoon.

His recital was greeted with laughter and even Will himself could enjoy it now that it was all past and he was once more safe in his room. For an hour Mr. Phelps remained in the room listening to the tales of the boys of their new life in the college, laughing as he heard of their pranks, and deeply interested in all they had to relate. At last when he arose to go to his room in the village hotel, he promised to come and attend church in the morning with the boys and then

explained that he would have two hours to spend with Will on the morning following as his train did not leave until half-past ten.
"But I have a recitation the first hour," said Will blankly. "I'll 'cut' it, though, for it isn't every day one has his daddy with him, and I wouldn't lose a minute of your time here, pop, for ten hours with old Splinter. I have Greek, you know, the first hour in the morning. Oh, I've got 'cuts' to burn," he added hastily as an unspoken protest appeared in the expression on his father's face. "You needn't worry about that."
"I don't want you to lose any recitation because I am here," said his father quietly. "I sha'n't want to come again if my coming interferes with your work, and as it is I have serious doubts—"
"All right, pop," replied Will patting his father affectionately on the shoulder. "I'll go to Splinter's class, though I know he'll 'go for' me too. I won't do a thing that'll ever keep you from showing up here in Winthrop again."
On Monday morning after the exercises in the chapel, Mr. Phelps went to Will's room and waited till the hour should pass and the eager-hearted boy should return. As the great clock in the tower rang out the hour he arose and stood in front of the window peering out across the campus at the building where Will was at work, but the stroke had scarcely ceased before he beheld the lad run swiftly down the steps and speed along the pathway toward his room as if he were running for a prize. The expression in the man's eyes was soft and there was also a suspicious moisture in them as well as he watched his boy. Was it only a dream or reality? Only a few short years ago and he had been an eager-hearted boy speeding over the same pathway (he smiled as he thought how the "speed" was never displayed on his way to the recitation building), and now it was his own boy who was sharing in the life of old Winthrop and doubtless he himself was in the minds of the young students relegated to that remote and distant period when the "old grads" were supposed to be young. Doubtless to them it was a time as remote as that when Homer's heroes contended in battle or the fauns and satyrs peopled the wooded hills and plains. And yet how vital it all was to him. He watched the groups of students moving across the campus, and as the sound of their shouts or laughter or the words of some song rose on the autumn air, it seemed to the man that he needed only to close his eyes and the old life would return—a life so like the present that it did not seem possible that a great gulf of thirty years lay between.
Mr. Phelps' meditations were interrupted by the entrance of Will, who burst into the room with the force of a small whirlwind.
"Here I am, pop!" he exclaimed as he tossed his books upon his couch and threw his cap to the opposite side of the room. "Old Splinter stuck me good this morning, but I can stand it as long as you are here."

"Who is Splinter?"
"Why, don't you know? I thought everybody knew Splinter. He's our professor of Greek and the biggest fraud in the whole faculty."
"What's the trouble with him?" Mr. Phelps spoke quietly but there was something in his voice that betrayed a deeper feeling and one that Will was quick to perceive and that gave him a twinge of uneasiness as well.
"Oh, he's hard as nails. He must have 'ichor' in his veins, not blood. I don't believe he ever was a boy. He must have been like Pallas Athenæ. Wasn't she the lady that sprang full-fledged from the brain of Zeus? Well, I've a notion that Splinter yelled in Greek when he was a baby. That is, if he ever was an infant, and called for his bottle in dactylic hexameter. Oh, I know lots about Greek, pop," laughed Will as his father smiled. "I know the alphabet and a whole lot of things even if Splinter thinks I don't."
"Doesn't he think you know much about your Greek?"
"Well, he doesn't seem to be overburdened with the weight of his opinion of me. He just looks upon me, I'm afraid, as if I was not a bright and shining light. 'Learn Greek or grow up in ignorance,' that's the burden of his song, and I've sometimes thought that about all the fun he has in life is flunking freshmen."
"How about the freshmen?"
"You mean me? Honestly, pop, I haven't done very well in my Greek; but I don't think it's all my fault. I've worked on it as I haven't worked on anything else in college. I've done my part, but Splinter doesn't seem to believe it. What am I going to do about it?"

Will in spite of his light-hearted ways, was seriously troubled and his father was silent for a brief time before he responded to the boy's question.

CHAPTER XI

THE PERPETUAL PROBLEM

"I was aware that you were having trouble with your Greek," said Mr. Phelps quietly, "and that was one of my reasons for stopping over here."

"You were? How did you know?"

"I had received word from the secretary of the faculty. He sent me a formal note announcing that your work was so low that it was more than probable you would fail in your mid-year examination."

For a moment Will Phelps was silent. His face became colorless and his heart seemed almost to rise in his throat. Fail in his mid-year's? A "warning" sent home to his father? To the inexperienced young student it seemed for a moment as if he was disgraced in the eyes of all his friends. He knew that his work had been of a low grade, but never for a moment had he considered it as being at all serious. So many of his newly formed friends in the college had been speaking of their conditions and low grades as a matter of course and had referred to them laughingly, much as if they were good jokes to be enjoyed that Will too had come almost to feel that his own trouble was not a serious one. And Splinter was the one to be blamed for the most of it, he was convinced. The words of his father, however, had presented the matter in an entirely different light, and his trouble was vastly increased by its evident effect upon him. Will's face was drawn and there was an expression of suffering upon it as he glanced again at his father and said:"What shall I do? Will it drop me out of college?"

"I think not necessarily. You must pass off more than half your hours to enable you to keep on with your class; but failure in one study will not bring that of itself, for your Greek is a four-hour course. But the matter is, of course, somewhat serious and in more ways than one."

"Yes, I know it," replied Will despondently.

"Well, if you know it, that's half the battle won already. The greatest trouble with most unsuccessful men is that they have never learned what their own weaknesses and limitations are. But you say you know, and I wish you'd tell me what you think the chief difficulty is."

"My Greek," said Will, trying to smile.

"But what's the trouble with the Greek?"

"The trouble is that the Greek troubles me. I suppose the Greek is all right and I'm all wrong."

"In what way?"

"I don't know it as I ought to."

"Is that 'Splinter's' fault?"

"No, it's mine. You know how hard I worked in the closing half of my last year in the high school, but that didn't, and I suppose couldn't, make up for what I hadn't done before."

"Are you working hard now?"

"On my Greek?"

"Yes."

"I'm putting more time on that than on everything else."

"I didn't ask you about the 'time,' but about the work.""Why, yes. I don't just see what you mean. I spend three hours on my Greek every day we have it."

"It's one thing to 'spend the time' and another to work. Some men will accomplish more in an hour than others will in three."

"I do my best," said Will gloomily. He felt almost as if his father was unfair with him and was disposed to question what he had said.

"Now, Will," said Mr. Phelps quietly, but in a tone of voice which his boy clearly understood, "it would be an easy thing for me to smooth over this matter and make light of it, but my love and interest in you are too strong to permit me to think of that for a moment. I believe in you, my boy, but there are some things in which I cannot aid you, some things which you must learn and do for yourself. Last year you faced your crisis as a man should, and I believe you will face this one too."

"It seems as if there was always something to be faced."

"There is. That's it, exactly. My boy, Splinter, as you call your professor in Greek, is not limited to the faculty of Winthrop College. In one form or another he presents himself all through your life. His name is simply that of the perpetual problem."

"I don't see, then—" interrupted Will.

"No, you don't see; but it is just because I do, and I am your father, that I am talking in this way. Why do you think I have sent you to college? It isn't for the name of it, or for the fun you will get out of it, or even for the friendships you will form here, though every one of these things is good in itself. It is to have you so trained, or rather for you so to train yourself, that when you go out from Winthrop you will be able to meet the very problems of which I am speaking and master them. They come to all, and the great difference in men is really in their ability to solve these very things. I think it is Emerson who says, 'It is as easy for a large man to do large things as it is for a small man to do small things.' And that is what I want for you, my boy, the ability to do the greater things."

"But I'll never use Greek any. I wish I could take some other study in its place."

"Just now it is not a question of Greek or something in its place. It is a question of facing and overcoming a difficulty or permitting it to overcome you. You must decide whether you will be a victor or a victim. There are just three things a man can do when he finds himself compelled to meet one of these difficult things that in one form or another come to everybody. He can turn and run from it, but that's the part of a coward. He can get around it, evade it somehow, but that's the part of the timid and palterer, and sooner or later the superficial man is found out. Then there is the best way, which is to meet and master it. Everybody has to decide which he will do, but do one of the three he must, and there is no escape."

"You think I ought to hit it between the eyes?"

"Yes, though I should not put it in quite that way," said his father with a smile.

"I'd like to smash it! I don't like it! I'll never make a Greek scholar, and I detest Splinter. He's as dry as a bone or a Greek root! He hasn't any more juice than a piece of boiled basswood!"

"That does not alter the matter. It won't change, and you've got to choose in which of the three ways I have suggested you will meet it."

"I suppose that's so," said Will quietly. "But it doesn't make it any easier."

"Not a bit."

"I know what you would say."

"Then it isn't necessary for me to say another word. There's one thing I am thankful for, Will, and that is that you and I are such good friends that we can talk this trouble all over together. The dean was telling me this morning—"

"Have you seen the dean?" interrupted Will quickly. "What did he say?"

"The dean was telling me," resumed Mr. Phelps smiling and ignoring the interruption, "that he sees so many of what might be termed the tragical elements of college life, that he sometimes feels as if he could not retain his position another day. Fathers and mothers broken-hearted, boys discouraged or worse, but the most tragical experience of all, he says, is to try to deal with fathers who have no special interest in their boys, and between whom there is no confidence. Whatever troubles may come to us, Will, I am thankful that that at least will not be one of them."

As he spoke Mr. Phelps arose, for the machine which was to convey him to the station could now be seen approaching and the time of his departure had arrived. His good-bye was hastily spoken for he knew how hard it would be for Will to be left behind, and in a brief time he had taken his seat in the auto. He saw Will as he hastily ran back to his room and then he could see him as he stood by the window in his room watching the departing auto as long as it could be seen. He gave no signal to show that he saw his boy, but his own eyes were wet as he was carried swiftly down the street, as he thought of the predicament in which Will was and how the testing-time had come again. But the young student must be left to fight out his battle alone. To save him from the struggle would be to save him from the strength. If it were only possible for a father to save his boy by assuming his burden, how thankful he would be, was Mr. Phelps' reflection, but he was too wise a man and too good a father to flinch or falter now, and, though his heart was heavy, he resolutely kept on his way leaving Will to fight his own battle, and hoping that the issue would be as he most fervently desired.

Left to himself, for a moment Will was almost despondent. The departure of his father seemed to leave the loneliness intensified, but he was recalled as he heard some one run up the stairway and rush into the room. His visitor was Mott, and perhaps the sophomore almost instinctively felt that his presence was not welcome, for he said:

"Governor gone, Phelps? Hope he left a good-sized check with you! I've come over to be the first to help you get rid of it."

"What's the trouble?" inquired Will quietly, glancing up as he spoke. "Your money all gone? Want to borrow some?"

"I'm always ready for that," laughed Mott, "though I'll have to own up that I've got a few cents on hand yet. No, I don't know that I want to borrow any; but I thought you might want a little help in getting rid of that check, and I'd just run over to oblige you. Just pure missionary work, you see." Mott seated himself in the large easy-chair and endeavored to appear at his ease, though to Will it still seemed as if there was something which still troubled his visitor.

"I haven't any special check."

"That's all right. My 'old man' never has been up to see me since I entered Winthrop, but as I look around at the fellows whose fathers and mothers have been up, I've noticed that they're usually pretty flush right after the old gentleman departs."

"Hasn't your mother ever been up?" inquired Will in surprise.

"No. Why should she? She hasn't any time to bother with me. She's on more than forty boards, and is on the 'go' all the time. She has to attend all sorts of 'mothers' meetings' too, and I believe she has a lecture also, which she gives."

"A lecture?"

"Yes. She has a lecture on 'The proper method of bringing up boys.' How do you suppose she ever has any time to visit me?" Mott laughed as if the matter was one of supreme indifference to him, but Will fancied that he could detect a feeling of bitterness beneath it all. For himself, the condition described by the sophomore seemed to him to be incredible. His own relations with his father had been of the frankest and most friendly nature. Indeed, it never occurred to him in a time of trouble or perplexity that there was any one else to whom he so naturally could go as to his own father. Since he had entered Winthrop, however, he had discovered several who were not unlike Mott in their feelings toward their own families; and as Mott spoke he almost unconsciously found a feeling of sympathy arising in his heart for him. Some of his apparently reckless deeds could be explained now.

"Mott, you must go home with me next vacation," he said impulsively.

"That's good of you, but it's too far off to promise. Say, Phelps, what's become of that man Friday of yours?"

"Who's he?"

"Schenck."

"Oh, he's flourishing."

"He's the freshest freshman that ever entered Winthrop. What do you suppose he had the nerve to say to me to-day?"

"I can't imagine."

"Well, he told me that he thought the Alpha Omega was the best fraternity in college, and that he'd made up his mind to join it."

As this was the fraternity to which Mott himself belonged, Will laughed as he said, "Oh, well, don't be too hard with Peter John. He doesn't know any better now, but he'll learn."

"That's what he will," replied Mott with a very decided shake of his head. "I thought I'd come over to tell you that the sophomore-freshmen meet is to come off on Saturday afternoon."

"Not next Saturday?" exclaimed Will aghast.

"Yes, that's the very day."

"They told me it wasn't to be for two weeks yet."

"All the same it's on Saturday. I thought I'd tell you, though I'm going to do my best to keep you from winning your numerals."

Mott rose and departed from the room, and when Foster returned he found his room-mate hard at work, with his Greek books spread out on the desk before him.

CHAPTER XII

THE MEET

The fact that the track meet between the two lower classes had been placed at an earlier date than that for which it had first been announced was a serious disappointment to Will Phelps. His success in the school athletics had made him quietly hopeful, if not confident, that he might be able to win some laurels in college, and he also was aware that the gold medal he wore upon his fob had made his own classmates expect great things from him. And the changed date now prevented him from doing any training and he must enter the contest without any preparation.

Reports had come to him that Mott and Ogden, the two fleetest-footed sophomores, had already been working hard, and rumors were also current that he himself was to be kidnapped and prevented from entering the games. Will had given but slight heed to any of these reports, but he had in his own mind decided that he would begin training at once for the contest, for if he should by any chance win then he would be the first member of his own class to gain the coveted privilege of wearing his class numerals upon his cap and sweater. And, not unnaturally, Will was eager to secure the honor.

As he thought over Mott's words he was half inclined to believe that the sophomore himself had been the cause of the unexpected change in the date of holding the games, and his feeling of anger and desire to win both became keener. There was no time, however, afforded in which he might make preparations for the meet, and he must simply do his best under existing circumstances. There was to be no burlesque or "horse play" in this contest, and the entire college would be on hand and interested to note the promise of the entering class in a department of college life that appealed strongly to all the students. Even his new determination to push his work in his Greek harder than ever he had done and his feeling of homesickness did not in the day that intervened between the present and the day of the games prevent his interest and excitement from increasing during the passing hours.

Saturday afternoon finally arrived, clear and cool, an ideal day for the contest. When Will stepped forth from the dressing-room, clad in his light running suit and with his bath robe wrapped around him, as he glanced over the track he could see that a crowd was already assembled. The sophomores were seated in a body in one portion of the "bleachers," and their noisy shouts or loud class cries rose steadily on the autumn air. Opposite was the freshman class, but its members were still too unfamiliar with their surroundings and with one another to enable them to join in anything like the unison of their rivals. In the grand stand were numbers of the members of the families of the faculty and the townspeople and visitors, and altogether the scene was one that strongly stirred Will and his room-mate, Foster Bennett, who also was to compete in the games.

Suddenly a loud, derisive shout arose from the sophomores, and Will glanced quickly up to discover its cause. In a moment the cause was seen, when Peter John Schenck came running across the field toward the place where Will and Foster were standing beside a few of their classmates, who were also waiting for the game to begin.

The sight of Peter John was one that caused even Will and Foster to smile, for their classmate was dressed as if he too was about to become a contestant, and this was something neither of them had expected. It was Peter John's garb, however, which had so greatly delighted the beholders, for it was unlike anything to be seen upon the field—"fearfully and wonderfully made," as Mott, who had joined them for a moment, had expressed it. Evidently it was the result of Peter John's own handiwork. His running trousers came to a place about halfway between his knees and ankles before they stopped, and were fashioned of coarse bagging or material very similar to it. He wore no running shoes, but a pair of gray woolen socks, plainly "hand made," provided a substitute. His "running shirt" was a calico blouse which had at one time doubtless served him as a garment in which he had done the daily chores upon his father's farm, but, as if to make matters still worse, a broad band of ribbon, the colors of the class, was diagonally fastened to his blouse in front, and Peter John's fierce shock of bright red hair, uncut since he had entered Winthrop, served to set off the entire picture he presented.

"Well, I guess we'll do 'em to-day, Will," exclaimed Peter John as he approached the group of which his friend was a member.

"I guess we will," remarked Mott soberly.

"I'm going to do my prettiest," continued Peter John.

"If you let anybody once get ahead of you, Schenck," said Mott, "you'll never catch him. If he sees you after him he'll run for his life."

"He'll have to!"

"What are you entered for?" inquired Mott, glancing at his program as he spoke.

"The half-mile run."

"Ever do it before?"

"Once or twice."

"What time did you make?"

"I don't just recollect."

"Never mind. You'll make a new record to-day."

"That's what I want to do," replied Peter John, sublimely unconscious that he was being made sport of by the sophomore.

The conversation was interrupted by the call, "All out for the hundred-yard dash!" and, as Will was to run in the first heat, he drew off his bath robe and tossing it to Foster, turned at once for the starting-place. He had already been indulging in a few trials of starting, but his feeling of confidence was by no means strong as he glanced at those who were to be his competitors. There were four runners in his heat, and one of them was Ogden, the sophomore of whose reputation as a "sprinter" Will already was aware. The other two were freshmen and therefore unknown quantities, but Will's chief interest was in Ogden. He could see the knots of muscles in his arms and back and legs, and his own feeling of confidence was in nowise strengthened by the sight. Certainly Ogden was a muscular fellow, and a competitor as dangerous as he was striking in his appearance.

The call, "On your marks," was given, and Will, with the other three, advanced and took his place on the line. Every nerve in his body seemed to be tingling with excitement and his heart was beating furiously.

"Get set!" called the starter, and then in a moment there followed the sharp report of the pistol and the runners were speeding down the course. Will felt that he had secured a good start, and but a few yards had been covered when he realized that he and Ogden were running almost side by side and had left the other two contestants behind them. Nor were their relative positions changed as they sped on down the track except that the distance between Will and Ogden and the two freshmen behind them was steadily increased. Will was dimly aware as he drew near the line that the entire sophomore body had risen and was noisily calling to their classmate to increase his speed. There was silence from the seats occupied by the freshman class, but Will was hardly mindful of the lack of support. Glancing neither to the right nor the left, he could almost instinctively feel that Ogden was a few inches in advance of him and all his efforts were centered upon cutting down the intervening distance.

As the contestants came within the last ten yards of the course, Will gathered himself together for one final burst of speed. His feet seemed scarcely to touch the ground as he darted forward. But Ogden was not to be outdone, for he too increased the pace at which he was running, and when they touched the line that was stretched across the course, the sophomore was still ahead by a few inches and had come in first in the heat, while Will was second.

Foster was standing near to catch his room-mate, and as he wrapped the bath robe around him, he said: "It's all right, Will; you're in the finals."

"First two taken?" gasped Will.

"Yes."

"Hold on. Let's hear the time," said Will, stopping abruptly as the announcer advanced.

"Hundred-yards dash, first heat," called the senior, "Won by number ten. Second, number fifteen. Time, ten and two-fifths seconds."

"That's good for the heat, Will," said Foster warmly.

"I'm not in training," said Will despondently.

"The others aren't either, or at least not much. You had Ogden nearly winded, and when it comes to the finals you'll do him up," said Foster encouragingly.

Will did not reply, for the call for the second heat was now made and he was intensely interested in watching Mott's performance, for his reputation in the college was even greater than Ogden's. And if he himself had been beaten by Ogden, what chance would he have against Mott? The question was not reassuring, but as the five men in the second heat could now be seen taking their positions on the line, it was for the moment ignored, as intensely interested he turned to watch the race that was about to be run.

In a moment the pistol was fired and the five contestants came speeding down the course. It was soon seen that Mott was leading, but only by a little, though he did not appear to be exerting himself strongly.

"Easy, dead easy!" Will heard a sophomore near him remark, and as he watched Mott's easy stride he heartily concurred in the opinion.

The runners were nearing the line now, and as Mott drew near he almost stopped for a moment and glanced smilingly behind him at his contestants. Instantly his nearest competitor darted forward and before the sophomore could recover himself he had touched the string and won the heat, with Mott a close second. Mott, however, appeared to be in nowise disconcerted and laughingly received the bantering words of his classmates. He laughed again when the time was announced as ten and four-fifths seconds, and approaching the place where Will and Foster were standing, said:

"You did well, freshman. Made better time than I did."

"I had to, if I kept anywhere near Ogden."

The other events of the meet were now being run off, and as Peter John Schenck took his place on the line for the half-mile run the uproar became almost tumultuous, and when the freshman apparently took it all in his most serious manner and bowed gravely to the sophomores, evidently appropriating to himself all the noisy demonstrations of delight, the shouts and laughter redoubled.

In a moment, however, the runners were off and Peter John quickly advanced to the first place, followed by a line of five that were well bunched together. There were many derisive calls and cries and Peter John's work seemed to be taken as a joke by all the spectators, who were loud in their declarations that he was "making a mistake" and would "never be able to maintain his stride." Around the course sped the runners until at last they were on the home stretch and still Peter John was in advance, his arms working like the fans of a Dutch windmill and his awkward movements becoming more awkward as the strain of the final part of the race came upon him. Still he was in the lead, however, and the derisive cries were giving place to shouts of approval and encouragement from his own classmates.

The increasing excitement seemed to provide an additional spur to the awkward freshman, for his speed suddenly increased and he darted across the line far in advance of his rivals who were bunched behind him. Laughter was mingled with the applause that greeted him, and when the captain of the college track team advanced and extended his hand in congratulation, the genuineness of the applause that followed was unquestioned.

Peter John, highly elated by his success, approached Will and said glibly: "There, Will, I rather guess that'll add five points to our score."

"I rather guess it will," laughed his classmate cordially. He was as greatly surprised as any one that day, but he was too generous to begrudge any praise to Peter John.

"Now see that you do as well," said Peter John, as the call for the finals in the hundred-yard dash was made.

Will made no response as he advanced to take his place. Foster had already won the running broad jump and was in a fair way to win the shot-put as well. Peter John had been successful too, and to Will it seemed that he must win his race or his disappointment would be almost too bitter to bear.

At the report of the pistol the contestants darted from the line and came speeding down the track toward the finish, which was near the place where the spectators were assembled. Vigorously, lusty, the perfection physically of young manhood, the four runners sped on with the swiftness of the wind, but when they touched the tape it was evident that Mott was first by a small margin and that Ogden was second, being an almost imperceptible distance in advance of Will Phelps, who had finished third in the race.

CHAPTER XIII

WAGNER'S ADVICE

The applause that greeted the winners was sounding but dimly and like some far-away shout in Will Phelps' ears when he staggered into the outstretched arms of Hawley, who was waiting to receive his classmate. Mortification, chagrin, disappointment were all mingled in his feelings, and it was all intensified by the fact that both Foster and Peter John had won their "numerals" and were now marked men in the class. Not that he begrudged either the honors he had won, but his own reputation as a sprinter had preceded his coming to Winthrop, and Will knew that great things had been expected of him.

"It was a great race, Phelps," said Hawley, "and you've added another point to our score."

Will could understand the attempt at consolation which his huge classmate was making, but it only served to increase the bitterness of his own defeat. He smiled, but made no response. He could see Peter John strutting about and receiving the half-bantering congratulations of the students, and his heart became still heavier.

"Never mind, Phelps, you didn't have any chance to train," said Hawley. "Mott and Ogden have been down on the track every evening for the past three weeks."

"They have?" demanded Will, a ray of light appearing for the moment."Sure. And besides all that they got the date of the 'meet' changed too."

"They beat me," said Will simply.

"Everybody expected them to. They all know you're a good runner, Phelps, but they say a freshman never wins. Such a thing hasn't been known for years. You see, a freshman is all new to it here, and I don't care how good he is, he can't do himself justice. You ought to hear what Wagner, the captain of the college track team, had to say about you."

"What did he say?" inquired Will eagerly.

"He said you had it in you to make one of the best runners in college, and he's going to keep an eye on you for the team too."

"Did he say that?"

"That's what he did."

"The two-twenty hasn't been run yet. I believe I'll go in for that."

"That's the way to talk."

"Let me see when it comes," said Will, turning to his program as he spoke.

"Fifteen minutes yet," said Hawley. "Come into the dressing room, Phelps, and I'll give you a good rubbing down."

Will at once accompanied his friend to the dressing room, and when the call for the two hundred and twenty yards' dash was made, he took his place on the line with the other competitors. There were only four, the same four that had run in the final heat of the hundred yards, the defeated contestants all having dropped out save one.

When the pistol was fired and the racers had started, Will was at once aware that again the victory was not to be his. The lack of training and practice, and perhaps also the depression which his previous defeat had produced in his mind contributed to his failure; but whatever the cause, though he exerted himself to the utmost, he found that he was unable to overtake either Mott or Ogden, who steadily held their places before him. It was true when the race was finished that he was less than a yard behind Mott, who was himself only about a foot in the rear of the fleet-footed Ogden, and that the fourth runner was so far behind Will that he was receiving the hootings and jibes of the sophomores, but still the very best that Phelps was able to do was to cross the line as third. It was true that again he had won a point for the honor of his class, but it was first place he had longed to gain, and his disappointment was correspondingly keen.

It was Hawley who again received him in his arms, and once more the young giant endeavored to console his defeated classmate, for as such Will looked upon himself, in spite of the fact that he had come in third, and therefore had scored a point in each race. But as Hawley perceived that his friend was in no mood to listen, he wisely refrained from speaking, and both stood near the track watching the contestants in the various events that were not yet run off. Too proud to acknowledge his disappointment in his defeat by departing from the field, and yet too sore in his mind to arouse much enthusiasm, he waited till the games were ended and it was known that the sophomores had won by a score of sixty-four and a half to forty-eight and a half. Then he quietly sought the dressing room, and as soon as he had donned his garments went at once to his own room.

It was a relief to find that not even Foster was there, and as he seated himself in his easy-chair and gazed out at the brilliantly clad hills with the purple haze that rested over them all, for a time a feeling of utter and complete depression swept over him. Was this the fulfillment of the dreams he had cherished of the happiness of his college life? Already warned by Splinter that his work in Greek was so poor that he was in danger of being dropped from the class, the keen disappointment of his father apparent though his words had been few, the grief in his home and the peril to himself were all now visible to the heart-sick young freshman. And now to lose in the two track events had added a weight that to Will seemed to be almost crushing. He had pictured to himself how he would lightly turn away his poor work in the classroom by explaining that he could not hope to win in everything, and that athletics had always been his strong point anyway. But now even that was taken away and his failure was almost equally apparent in both.

He could see Peter John coming up the walk, receiving the congratulations of the classmates he met and giving his "pump-handle" handshake to those who were willing to receive it. It was maddening and almost more than Will thought he could bear. It was a mistake that he had ever come to college anyway, he bitterly assured himself. He was not well prepared in spite of the fact that he had worked hard for a part of his final year in the preparatory school. Greek? He detested the subject. Even his father came in for a share of blame, for if he had not insisted upon his taking it Will never would have entered Splinter's room. He might have taken German under "Dutchy," or English under Professor Jones, as many of his classmates were doing, and every one declared that the work there was a "snap."

It was not long before Will Phelps was in a state of mind wherein he was convinced that he was being badly treated and had more to contend against than any other man in his class. His naturally impulsive disposition seldom found any middle ground on which he was permitted to stand. His father had one time laughingly declared that the comparative degree had been entirely left out of Will's make-up and that things were usually of the superlative. "Worst," "best," "poorest," "finest" were adjectives most commonly to be found in his vocabulary, and between the two extremes a great gulf appeared to be fixed. He had also declared that he looked for Will to occupy no middle ground. He would either be a pronouncedly successful man or an equally pronounced failure, a very good man or a man who would be a villain. And Will had laughingly accepted the verdict, being well assured that he knew, if it must be one of the two, which it would of necessity be. All things had gone well with him from the time of his earliest recollections. His home had been one of comfort and even of elegance, any reasonable desire had never been denied, he had always been a leading spirit among the pupils of the high school, and that he was too, a young fellow who was graceful in his appearance, well dressed, and confident of his own position, doubtless Will Phelps was aware, although he did not give expression to the fact in such terms.

And now the "superlative degree" had certainly displayed itself, Will thought in his wretchedness, only it had manifested itself in the extreme which he never had before believed to be possible with him. He listened to the shouts and laughter of the students passing along the street below and every fresh outburst only served to deepen his own feeling of depression. Not any of the enthusiasm was for him.

He was roused from his bitter reflection by the opening of the door into his room, but he did not look up, as he was convinced that it was only his room-mate, and Foster understood him so well that he would not talk when he saw that he was in no mood for conversation.

"Hello, Phelps! What's wrong?"

Will hastily sat erect and looked up. His visitor was Wagner, the captain of the track team, the one senior of all others for whom Will cherished a feeling of respect that was almost unbounded. He had never met the great man before, but he had looked up to him with awe when Wagner had been pointed out to him by admiring students, and he was aware that the captain's reputation was as great in the college for his manliness as it was for his success in athletics. Unpretentious, straightforward, without a sign of "cant" or "gush" about him, the influence of the young leader had been a mighty force for good in the life of Winthrop College. And now as Will glanced into the face of the tall, powerful young fellow and realized that it was indeed himself whom his visitor was addressing, his feeling of depression instantly gave place to surprise and in the unexpected honor he found it difficult to express himself.

"Nothing much. I wasn't just looking for any—for you," he stammered. "Won't you take this chair, Mr. Wagner?" Will pushed the easy-chair toward his visitor as he spoke and again urged him to be seated.

"That's all right, Phelps. Keep your seat. I'll just sit here," replied Wagner, seating himself upon the edge of Will's desk. "How do you feel after the games?" he inquired.

"I'm a bit sore outside and worse still inside."

"What's the trouble?"

"I came in only third."

"Only third? Where did you expect to come in?"

"Why—why, I was hoping I'd get first in the hundred," Will managed to reply.

"You're a modest youth," laughed Wagner, surveying his long legs and laughing in such a manner that Will was compelled to join.

"Well, the fellows rather thought I'd win and that's what makes me feel worse about it."

"They're only freshmen; they don't know any better," laughed Wagner. "Don't let that bother you for a minute. I think you did well myself, and besides, the freshmen very seldom win in the sprints. I don't know that I ever saw one since I've been in college."

"Did you win the hurdles when you were a freshman?""Oh, I just happened to. 'Twas an accident of some kind, I fancy. Yes, I think the soph who was ahead of me tripped and fell, so I crawled in first."

"That will do for you to tell."

"Perhaps I did win. But that's neither here nor there. It isn't what I came for. I didn't want to talk about myself but about you."

Will looked up eagerly but did not speak, though his question was to be seen in the expression of his face.

"My advice to you is to go to work and try for the track team in the spring."

"Do you think I can make it?" said Will breathlessly.

"I don't say that," laughed Wagner. "That's something to be decided later. All I said was that you'd better 'try' for it. You've nothing to lose if you fail and something to win if you succeed."

"But if I should try and then not make it."

"Yes, that's a possibility, of course. No man can ever tell about that. But I shouldn't let it break my heart if I didn't make the team the first year. Very few do that. All I say is go ahead and try. No man can ever tell what's in him till he tests himself, can he?"

"No, I suppose not."

"Now don't have any nonsense about it, Phelps, and don't misunderstand me. I believe in every man doing his best and then just resting there and not crying over what he can't ever have. If a man does his best and then doesn't have the whole world bowing and scraping before him because he isn't very high up, that isn't any reason why he should kick. Take what you've got, use it, test it, and then if you find you're not a star but only a candle, why, just shine as a candle and don't go sputtering around because you can't twinkle like a star. At least that's the way I look at it."

"Perhaps a fellow's father and mother don't look at it that way."

"Are you having trouble with Splinter?" demanded the senior sharply.

"A little. Yes, a good deal. I detest the fellow!" said Will bitterly.

"No wonder you lost the hundred," responded Wagner with a smile. "Do you know, Phelps, I had the same experience you're having with him when I was a freshman."

"What did you do?"

"Do? There's only one thing to do and that is to do his work. But I advise you to go down to his house and see him and talk it over."

"He won't want to see me."

"Yes, he will. He's not half so bad as you think. Try it; I did."

"He'll think I'm trying to boot-lick."

"No, he won't. You can run if you have to, can't you?" demanded Wagner. "You've got a good stride, and, like trying for the track team, you've nothing to lose and everything to gain."

CHAPTER XIV

THE ADVICE FOLLOWED

For a time after the departure of Wagner, Will Phelps sat thinking over the stirring words of his visitor. His feeling of positive discouragement, with the natural rebound of his impulsive temperament, had in a measure given place to one of confidence and even of elation. To be recognized by the great captain was an honor of itself, but to receive a personal visit from him and a warm invitation to try for a place on the track team was a distinction for which he never had even dared to dream. Even his other pressing problem—his work in Greek—appeared slightly more rosy-hued now, and a sudden determination seized upon him to do as Wagner had suggested and see Splinter that very night.

Accordingly, soon after dinner—the meal at his fraternity house which he had dreaded in view of the semi-defeat of the afternoon—he started toward the home of his professor of Greek, resolved to talk over the entire situation with him and strive to learn exactly where he stood and what his prospects were likely to be.

As he approached the walk that led from the street back to the professor's home he came face to face with Mott and Peter John Schenck. His surprise at meeting them was not greater than that he should find them together, and the fact to his mind boded little good for his classmate.

"Going in to see Splinter?" inquired Mott.

"Yes.""Better not."

"Why?"

"Boot-licking isn't in very high favor here at Winthrop."

Will was glad that the darkness concealed the flush which he knew crept over his face, but his voice was steady as he replied: "That's all right, Mott. I'm not going in to see Splinter because I want to, you may let your heart rest easy as to that."

"How long are you going to be in the house?"

"I'm afraid that will not be for me to decide. If I have my way, it won't be long."

"Well, good luck to you!" called Mott as he and his companion passed on down the street.

Will rang the bell and was at once ushered into the professor's study. The professor himself was seated at his desk with a green shade over his eyes, and evidently had been at work upon some papers. Will even fancied that he could recognize the one which he himself had handed in the preceding day and his embarrassment increased.

"Ah, good evening, Mr. Phelps," said the professor extending his hand and partly rising from his seat as he greeted his caller. "Will you be seated?"

"Good evening, professor," replied the freshman as he took the chair indicated.

An awkward silence followed which Will somehow found it difficult to break in upon. He heartily wished that he had not come, for the reality was much worse than he had thought. Even the very lines and furrows in the professor's face seemed to him to be forbidding, and he felt that it would be well-nigh impossible for him to explain the purpose of his coming.

"Was there something concerning which you desired to consult me?" inquired the professor. The voice seemed to be as impersonal as that of a phonograph, and every letter in every word was so distinctly pronounced that the effect was almost electric.

"Yes, sir."

Again silence intervened. The professor's lips moved slightly as if, as Will afterwards declared, "he was tasting his Greek roots," but he did not speak. The freshman shifted his position, toyed with his gloves and at last, unable to endure the suspense any longer, he broke forth:

"Yes, sir, there is, professor. I have not been doing very well in my Greek."

"Ah. Let me see." The professor opened a drawer and drew forth a little notebook which he consulted for a brief time. "Yes, you are correct. Your work is below the required standard."

"But what am I to do about it?" demanded Will.

"Yes, ah, yes. I fancy it will be necessary for you to spend a somewhat longer period of study in preparation."

"But how shall I study?"

"Yes. Yes. Ah, yes. Exactly so. So you refer to the method to be employed in the preparation for the classroom?"

"Yes, sir. That's it. I'm willing enough to work, but I don't know how."

"Well, I should say that the proper method would be to employ a tutor for a time. There are several very excellent young gentlemen who are accustomed to give their services to deserving youth—"

"I don't want them to give it. I'll pay for it!" interrupted Will.

"I was about to say that these young gentlemen give their services for a consideration—a proper consideration—of course."

The professor's thin lips seemed to be reluctant to permit the escape of a word, so firmly were they pressed together during the intervals between his slowly spoken words. His slight figure, "too thin to cast a shadow," in the vigorous terms of the young freshman, was irritating in the extreme, and if Will had followed his own inclinations he would at once have ended the interview.

"I knew I could get a tutor, and if it is necessary I'll do it. But I did not know but that you might be able to make a suggestion to me. I know I'm not very well prepared, but if you'll give me a show and tell me a little how to go to work at the detestable stuff I'll do my best. I don't like it. I wouldn't keep at it a minute if my father was not so anxious for me to keep it up and I'd do anything in the world for him. That's why I'm in the Greek class."

"You are, I fancy (fawncy was the word in the dialect of the professor) doing better work in the various other departments than in your Greek?"

"Yes, sir. I think so."

"You are not positive?"

"Yes, sir. I know I'm doing fairly well in my Latin and mathematics. Why the recitation in Latin never seems to be more than a quarter of an hour, while the Greek seems as if it would never come to an end. I think Professor Baxter is the best teacher I ever saw and he doesn't make the Latin seem a bit like a dead language. But the Greek seems as if it had never been alive."

"Ahem-m!" piped up the thin voice of the professor of Greek.

Will Phelps, however, was in earnest now and his embarrassment was all forgotten. He was expressing his own inward feelings and without any intention or even thought of how the words would sound he was describing his own attitude of mind. He certainly had no thought of how his words would be received.

"Ahem-m!" repeated the professor shrilly and shifting a trifle uneasily in his seat. "I fawncy that a student always does better work in a subject which he enjoys."

"Yes, but doesn't he enjoy what he can do better work in too? Now I don't know how to study Greek, can't seem to make anything out of it. As you told me one day in the class 'I make Greek of it all.' Perhaps not exactly the kind of Greek you want, though," Will added with a smile.

"Ah, yes. I fawncy a trifle more of work would aid you."

"Of course! I know it would! And that's what I'm willing to do and what I want to do, professor. But the trouble is I don't know just how to work."

"I—I fail to see precisely what you mean."

"Why, I spend time enough but I don't seem to 'get there'—I mean I don't seem to accomplish much. My translation's not much good, and everything is wrong.""Perhaps you have an innate deficiency—"

"You mean I'm a fool?" Will laughed good-naturedly, and even the professor smiled.

"Ah, no. By no means, Mr. Phelps, quite the contrary to that, I assure you. There are some men who are very brilliant students in certain subjects, but are very indifferent ones in others. For example, I recollect that some twenty years ago—or to be exact nineteen years ago—there was a student in my classes who was very brilliant, very brilliant indeed. His name as I recall it was Wilder. So proficient was he in his Greek that some of the students facetiously called him Socrates, and some still more facetious even termed him Soc. I am sure, Mr. Phelps, you have been in college a sufficient length of time to apprehend the frolicsome nature of some of the students here."

"I certainly have," Will remarked with a smile, recalling his own compulsory collar-button race.

"I fawncied so. Well, this Mr. Wilder to whom I refer was doing remarkable work, truly remarkable work in Greek, but for some cause his standing in mathematics was extremely low, and in other branches he was not a brilliant success."

"What did he do?" inquired Will eager to bring the tedious description to a close, and if possible receive the suggestions for which he had come.

"My recollection is that he finally left college."

"Indeed!" Will endeavored to be duly impressed by the startling fact, but as he recalled the professor's statement that the brilliant Wilder was in college something like twenty years before this time, his brilliancy in being able to complete the course and now be out from the college did not seem to him to indicate any undue precocity on the part of the aforesaid student.

"Yes, it was so. It has been my pleasure to receive an annual letter from him, and I trust you will not think I am unduly immodest when I state that he acknowledges that all his success in life is due to the work he did here in my own classes in Winthrop. My sole motive in referring to it is the desire to aid you."

"You think I may be another Wilder?" inquired Will lightly.

"Not exactly. That was not the thought that was uppermost. But it may serve as an incentive to you."

"What is this Wilder doing now?"

"Ahem-m!" The professor cleared his throat repeatedly before he spoke. "He is engaged in an occupation that brings him into contact with the very best that has been thought and said, and also into contact with some of the brightest and keenest intellects of our nation."

"He must be an editor or a publisher then."

"Not exactly. Not exactly, Mr. Phelps. He is engaged rather in a mercantile way, though with the most scholarly works, I do assure you."

"Is he a book agent?"

"Ahem-m! Ahem-m! That is an expression I seldom use, Mr. Phelps. It has become a somewhat obnoxious term, though originally it was not so, I fawncy. I should hardly care to apply that expression as indicative of Mr. Wilder's present occupation.""And you think if I try hard I may at last become a book agent too?"

"You have mistaken my implication," said the professor scowling slightly as he spoke. "I was striving solely to provide an incentive for you. You may recall what Homer, or at least he whom in our current phraseology we are accustomed to call Homer—I shall not now enter into the merits of that question of the Homeridæ. As I was about to remark, however, you doubtless may recollect what Homer in the fifth book of his Iliad, line forty-ninth, I think it is, has to say."

"I'm afraid I don't recall it. You see, professor, I had only three books of the Iliad before I came to Winthrop."

"Surely! Surely! Strange that I should have forgotten that. It is a pleasure you have in store then, Mr. Phelps."

"Can you give me any suggestions how to do better work, professor?" inquired Will mildly.

"My advice to you is to secure Mr. Franklin of the present junior class to tutor you for a time."

"Thank you. I'll try to see him to-night," said Will rising and preparing to depart.

"That might be wise. I trust you will call upon me again, Mr. Phelps. I have enjoyed this call exceedingly. You will not misunderstand me if I say I had slight knowledge of your classic tastes before, and I am sure that I congratulate you heartily, Mr. Phelps. I do indeed."

"Thank you," replied Will respectfully, and he then departed from the house. He was divided between a feeling of keen disappointment and a desire to laugh as he walked up the street toward his dormitory. And this was the man who was to stimulate his intellectual processes! In his thoughts he contrasted him with his professor in Latin, and the man as well as the language sank lower and lower in his estimation. And yet he must meet it. The problem might be solved but could not be evaded. He would see Franklin at once, he decided.

CHAPTER XV

A REVERSED DECISION

In the days that immediately followed, Will Phelps found himself so busy that there was but little time afforded for the pleasures of comradeship or for the lighter side of college life. Acting upon the one good point in the advice of his professor of Greek he secured a tutor, and though he found but little pleasure in the study, still he gave himself to it so unreservedly that when a few weeks had elapsed, a new light, dim somewhat, it was true, and by no means altogether cheering, began to appear upon his pathway. It was so much more difficult to catch up than to keep up, and perhaps this was the very lesson which Will Phelps needed most of all to learn. There was not much time given to recreation now, and Will acting upon the advice of the instructor in athletics had abandoned his projected practice in running though his determination to try to secure a place on the track team was as strong as ever. But he had substituted for the running a line of work in the gymnasium which tended to develop the muscles in his legs and keep his general bodily condition in good form. He was informed that success in running was based upon nerve force as well as upon muscular power, and that "early to bed" was almost as much a requisite here as it was in making a man "healthy and wealthy and wise." This condition however he found it exceedingly difficult to fulfill, for the additional work he was doing in Greek made a severe draught upon his time as well as upon his energies."I hate the stuff!" he declared one night to his room-mate after he had spent several hours in an almost vain effort to fasten certain rules in his mind. "You don't catch me taking it after this year."

"You don't have to look ahead, Will," suggested Foster kindly.

"No, the look behind is bad enough. If I had worked in the early part of the high-school course as I ought to I'd not be having all this bother now."

"And if you work now you won't have the trouble ahead," laughed Foster.

"I suppose that's the way of it."

"Of course it is. A fellow reaps what he sows."

"I'd rather rip what I sewed," said Will ruefully. "Do you know, Foster, sometimes I think the game isn't worth the candle. I'd give it all up, even if I had to leave college, if it wasn't for my father."

"You wouldn't do anything of the kind and you know it, Will Phelps! You're not the fellow to run when the pinch comes."

"I'd like to, though," said Will thoughtfully. "My fit in Greek was so poor I'll never get much of the good from studying it."

"You'll be all the stronger for not giving up, anyway."

"That's the only thing that keeps me at it. I'm so busy I don't even have time to be homesick."

"Well, that's one good thing."

"Perhaps it is, but if I flunk out at the mid-year's—"

"You won't if you only keep it up and keep at it."

"I'd feel better if I thought I wouldn't.""You'll be all right," said Foster soothingly, for he understood his friend so well that he knew he was in one of his periods of mental reaction, and that what he needed was encouragement more than anything else.

"And just think of it," continued Will gloomily, "you're about the only one of the fellows I ever see nowadays. I don't believe I've seen Hawley in three weeks, that is to have a word with him."

"Who has?"

"I don't know. All the fellows, I suppose."

"Not much! Hawley is working like a Trojan on the football team. You know that as well as I do."

"I suppose that's so. Still I'd like to see the fellow once in a while."

"He's a good man all right and I've a notion that he's saved Peter John from more than one scrape because he roomed with him."

"I haven't seen Peter John either for more than a week."

"We ought to look him up and keep an eye on him."

"'Keep an eye on him'? You want to keep both eyes and your hands and your feet too, for the matter of that. He certainly is the freshest specimen I ever saw, and the worst of it all is that he doesn't seem to know that he lacks anything. He's just as confident when he marches up to Wagner and gives him some points in running the track team as he is when he's telling you and me how to work up our Greek. And the fellow has flunked in Greek every time he's been called up for the past ten days.""Yes, I know it. That's why I said we ought to look out for him."

"He's got to learn how to look out for himself."

"He needs a tutor, though, Will—"

"Same as I do in my Greek? That's not nice of you, Foster. It's bad enough to have to work up the stuff without having it rubbed in. And yet," said Will quietly, "I suppose I am in the same box with Peter John. He doesn't know some things and I don't know others."

"No one has everything," said Foster quickly.

"Startling fact! But we fellows who live in glass houses mustn't throw stones I 'fawncy,' as my learned instructor would put it. There I am again, finding fault even with Splinter when I ought to be boning on this Greek to make up for my own lacks. Here I go!" And Will resolutely turned to the books which were lying open on his desk.

The silence that reigned in the room was broken in a few minutes when Hawley opened the door and entered. His coming was greeted enthusiastically, and when he had accepted the invitation to be seated, he said quickly, "I can't stay, fellows."

"You never can nowadays, Hawley. Since you've been on the team you've shaken all your old friends."

"You'd shake too, if you had the captain over you that we have."

"Is he hard?"

"Hard? He beats every coach we've got. He goes into the game as if there wasn't anything else to think of."

"It counts though," responded Will emphatically. "We haven't lost but two games so far this season, and they were with —— and ——. Of course we couldn't expect to win those."

"Oh, we've done fairly well. But the hardest rub is coming next Saturday. That's when we're going down to the city to have our game with Alden. There'll be a big crowd out, and the Alden alumni are mighty strong around town there too, and they'll be out in bunches. We've got to keep up our end, and that's why I've come over to see you fellows. I want you both to go next Saturday."
"Sure!" shouted Will, leaping to his feet. "We'll be on hand. You rest your soul easy about that."
"How many are going, Hawley?" inquired Foster quietly.
"So far, about half the college have agreed to go. We'd like to get another hundred to go along. It will make a big difference to the team. Last year there were six thousand people on the grounds, and it rained hard too, all the time. This year, if we have a good day, there'll be ten thousand on hand anyway."
"How are the fellows going down?" said Foster.
"Chartered a special train."
"What's the fare?"
"About six dollars for the round trip."
"Come back the same day?"
"Can if you want to, the train is coming back that night after the game. But a good many will stay over till Monday."
"When do you have to know?"
"You ought to give in your names by to-morrow night. Peter John is going along. I think he'll be a good mascot, don't you?" laughed Hawley."I'm sorry Peter John is going," said Foster thoughtfully.
"Sorry!" exclaimed Hawley aghast. "Why, man alive, he'll have the time of his life."
"That's what I'm afraid of, and besides he ought not to spend the money."
"I don't know anything about that," said Hawley quickly. "But he may make enough on the game to pay all his expenses."
"Has he staked money on the game?" said Will.
"You'll have to ask him," retorted Hawley somewhat sharply. "We can count on you two fellows then, can we?"
"That's what you can!" replied Will heartily.
"I'll think about it and let you know in the morning," said Foster. And Hawley at once departed from the room.
"What do you suppose it means that Peter John is going?" was Foster's first question after their visitor had departed.
"I don't know, but I don't like the look of it," responded Will.
"Neither do I. Can we do anything to stop it?"
"No, I'm afraid not. Peter John is getting beyond us."

Foster shook his head thoughtfully but made no response, and the work was resumed. For an hour each boy labored at his desk, and then Foster was the first to break in upon the silence.

"Will," he said, "I think I'll go with you on that trip with the team."

"I don't think I'll go," said Will quietly."Not go? Why not?" demanded Foster in astonishment.

"I've been thinking it over and I've made up my mind that it won't do for me to break in on the regular program I've mapped out for myself. You see Saturday is the day when I always have a double dose with my tutor, and it won't do for me to spoil it," and Will Phelps made a wry face as he spoke.

"But, Will," protested Foster, "you can make up the work before then and not lose a bit."

"Yes, I've thought of that, but I don't think I'll do it. It's a bitter dose I know, but I might as well swallow it first as last."

"Do you mean it?"

"Don't I act as if I did?"

"All right. I'll not say another word. Maybe it'll be a way out for Peter John. I'd like to fix it for the fellow if I can."

"I don't just see—" began Will; but he stopped when he perceived that his room-mate had risen from his seat and was about to depart from the room.

On the following day the excitement among the students of Winthrop increased when a mass meeting was held and various leading spirits of the college delivered very florid and perfervid addresses in which the student-body was urged to support the team and take advantage of the low rates offered to accompany it and be on hand on the field to cheer it on to victory. Shouts and cheers greeted the speakers, and when the meeting broke up and the boys were returning to their rooms Mott and Peter John joined Will on his way to Perry Hall."Have the time of your young life on Saturday, Phelps," said Mott loudly.

"I'm not going."

"Why not? All the fellows are."

"I'd like to, but I've some work I must do, and I can't break in on it."

"You must be a 'shark' Phelps," laughed Mott. "I'd like to see the work that would keep me away. Peter John Schenck and I intend to take it all in, don't we, freshman?" he added, turning to his companion as he spoke.

"Ye-es, I guess so," responded that worthy who had been addressed.

"You'll have a good time," said Will. "I wish I could go too, but I can't, and the only thing for me to do is to stand up and not whine over it."

"You'll be sorry for it," laughed Mott, as he and Peter John turned toward the latter's room. "All we can do will be to try to make up for what you're going to lose."

And Will Phelps did almost feel that he was too strict in his demands upon himself when the student-body formed in line early Saturday morning and, preceded by a band, started down the street on the way to the station. His room-mate had said no more to him concerning the trip, but as Will marched by Foster's side he could feel the deep sympathy of his friend. His heart almost misgave him. It was not too late even yet to go, for doubtless he could borrow money of some one. Perhaps it was too much a mere sentiment to hold himself to his work as he was doing. And he detested the work so heartily too.Still he held rigidly to his decision, and even when the heavily laden train pulled out from the station and the words of the song which was sung came back to him he did not falter, though his heart was heavy within him.

Gaudeamus igiturJuvenes dum sumusGaudeamus igiturJuvenes dum sumusPost jucundam juventutemPost molestam senectutemNos habebit humusNos habebit humus.

CHAPTER XVI

TELEGRAMS

When Will Phelps returned to the college, the entire place to him seemed to be deserted, and a stillness rested over all that was almost oppressive. Even the few college boys who were to be seen about the grounds all shared in the prevailing gloom and increased the sense of loneliness in the heart of the young freshman. When he entered his room, the sight of his room-mate's belongings was almost like that of the possessions of the dead and Will Phelps was utterly miserable and dejected.

Work he decided was his only cure and at once he busied himself at his task from which he was aroused in the course of an hour or two by the coming of the senior who was tutoring him.

"I'm mighty glad to see you," said Will impulsively. "I feel as if I was about the only one of my kind in the world."

"You're downhearted over deciding to stay in town, to-day?" replied his tutor pleasantly. "Oh, well, never mind. It will be a good tonic for you and when you've passed your mid-year's in Greek, you'll never once think of this trip with the team to-day."

"I'm afraid that's cold comfort just at the present moment. I've just been hanging on and that's all there is to it."

"Sometimes it's the only thing a fellow can do. It may bring a lot of other good things with it, though."

"Maybe," replied Will dubiously. "There's one thing I've learned though, and if I ever come to know my Greek as well as I know that, I'll pass all right."

"What's that?"

"Never to get behind. I'll keep up and not catch up. When I see what a fool I made of myself in my 'prep' days, I wonder sometimes that I ever got into college anyway. I never really worked any except in a part of the last year."

"You're working now," suggested the senior.

"Yes, I have to. I don't like it though. The descent to Avernus is the easy trip, if I remember my Virgil correctly. It's the getting back that's hard."

"Do you know, I never just believed that."

"You didn't? Why not? Why, you can see it every day! It's just as easy as sliding down hill. It's dragging the sled back up the hill that makes the trouble."

"That isn't quite a fair illustration. If I'm not mistaken, it seems to me that somewhere, sometime, some one said that 'The way of the transgressor is hard.' He didn't seem to agree with Virgil's statement somehow, did he?"

"But that means it's hard afterward."

"That isn't what it says. I think it means just what it says too."

"I don't see."

"Well, to me it's like this. In every fellow there's a good side and a bad side. Sort of a Doctor Jekyl and Mr. Hyde in every one of us. I heard the other day in our laboratory of a man who had taken and grafted one part of the body of an insect on the body of another. He tried it both on the chrysalis and on an insect too. I understood that he took the pupa of a spider and by very careful work grafted upon it the pupa of a fly. Think of what that monstrosity must have been when it passed out from the chrysalis and became a full-fledged living being. One part of it trying to get away from the other. One wanting to fly and the other to hide. One part wanting to feed on flies and the other part in mortal terror of all spiders."

"Was that really so?" inquired Will deeply interested.

"I didn't see it myself, but it was told over in the biological laboratory and I don't think there was any question about it. It struck me that it was just the way some of us seem to be built, a sort of a spider and fly combination and not the ordinary combination either, when the fly is usually inside of the spider and very soon a part of his majesty. And yet when you've told all that you know, it's a sort of monstrosity after all, and that the truth is that a fellow really is his best self if he'll only give that part half a chance. That's why I say the way of the transgressor is hard and not easy. A fellow is going against the grain of his best side. He throws away his best chances under protest all the while, and he doesn't want to do it either. No, Phelps, I believe if a fellow goes down hill it's like a man dragging a balky horse. It looks easy but it isn't, and he himself is pulling against it all the time."

"I never thought of it in that way before."

"Then on the other hand this very kind of work you're doing now is the sort that stirs your blood. I expect that those fellows who live down in the tropics and about all the work they have to do to feed themselves is to pick a banana off a tree and go through the exertion of peeling it, don't really get half the fun out of life that some of us boys had up on the hillside farms in Vermont. Why, when we'd have to get up winter mornings, with the weather so cold that we'd have to be all the while on the lookout that we didn't freeze our ears or noses, and when we'd have to shovel out the paths through three feet of snow and cut the wood and carry water to the stock, it did seem at times to be a trifle strenuous; but really I think the boys in Vermont get more fun out of life than the poor chaps in the tropics do who plow their fields by just jabbing a hole in the ground with their heel, and when they plant, all they have to do is to just stick a slip in the ground. It's the same way here, Phelps. This sort of thing you're doing is hard, no doubt about that; but it's the sort of thing that really stirs up a live man, after all."

"I'm afraid I'll be all stirred up if we don't get at this work pretty soon," laughed Will, who was nevertheless deeply impressed by the words he had heard from the prospective valedictorian of the senior class. "Why can't we do it all up this morning?" he inquired eagerly.

"All?"

"Oh, I mean all we were planning to do to-day. I'd like to go down to the gym this afternoon and watch the bulletins of the game. I decided not to go, but if I can get my work off that'll be the next best thing; and besides it'll help to pass the time. It's going to be a long day for me."

"All right, I'm agreeable," replied the senior cordially.

Until the hour of noon was rung out by the clock in the tower, Will labored hard. The words of his tutor had been inspiring, but he could not disguise from himself the fact, however, that he had little love for the task. It was simply a determination not to be "downed," as Will expressed it, that led him on and he was holding on doggedly, resolutely, almost blindly, but still he was holding on. About three o'clock in the afternoon the few students who were in town assembled at the telegraph office where messages were to be received from the team at intervals of ten minutes describing the progress of the game. One of the seniors had been selected to read the dispatches and only a few minutes had elapsed after the assembly had gathered before the senior appeared, coming out of the telegraph office and waving aloft the yellow slip. A cheer greeted his appearance but this was followed by a tense silence as he read aloud:

"They're off. Great crowd. Winthrop line outweighed ten pounds to a man. Holding like a stone wall."

"That's the way to talk it!" shouted the reader as he handed the dispatch to the operator, and then began to sing one of the college songs, in which he was speedily joined by the noisy group.

The song was hushed when again the operator appeared and handed another slip to the leader. Glancing quickly at it the senior read aloud:"Ball on Alden's twenty-five yard line. Great run by Thomas. Hawley playing star game."

Hawley, Thomas, and the captain of the team, and then the team itself, were cheered, and once more the group of students gave vent to their feelings in a noisy song. It was all stimulating and interesting, and Will Phelps was so keenly alive to all that was occurring, that for the time even his disappointment in not being able to accompany the team was forgotten.

A groan followed the reading of the next dispatch. "Alden's ball on a fumble. Steadily forcing Winthrop line back by superior weight. Ball on Winthrop's forty-yard line."

"That looks bad," said Will's tutor, who had now joined the assembly and was standing beside Will Phelps. "We've a quick team, but I'm afraid of Alden's weight. They've two or three men who ought not to be permitted to play, anyway."

"Professionals?" inquired Will.

"Yes, or worse."

"Have we any on our team?"

"Hardly," laughed the senior. But Will was thinking of the conversation he had had with Hawley when they had first entered college, and was silent. Besides, another dispatch was about to be read and he was eager to hear.

"Ball on Winthrop's five-yard line. Hawley injured and out of the game."

"Too much beef," muttered the reader disconsolately, and the silence in the assembly was eloquent of feelings that could not be expressed.

Less than the regular interval had elapsed when another yellow slip was handed to the reader, and the suspense in the crowd was almost painful. The very silence and the glances that were given were all indicative of the fear that now possessed every heart.

"Alden makes touchdown. No goal," read the leader.

"Six nothing! Team's no good this year, anyway!" declared one of the students angrily. "Had no business to play Alden, anyway! Ought to have games with teams in our class."

"Alden seemed to be in our class last year, or rather she didn't," said the reader quietly. "Remember what the score was?"

"No. What was it?"

"Twenty-four to nothing in our favor. If they win this year it will be only following out the regulation see-saw that's been going on for seven years. Neither college has won its game for two successive years."

"Alden will win this time all right enough."

"Perhaps. The game isn't ended yet. You haven't learned the Winthrop spirit yet, which is never to give up till the game is played clear through to the end. You've got something to learn yet." The rebuked student did not reply, but the expression upon his face betrayed the fact that he was still unconvinced, and that he did indeed have the first of all lessons taught at Winthrop yet to learn.

The score was unchanged at the end of the first half, and the students scattered during the period of intermission, assured that no further information would be received until after the second half of the game was begun. The confidence in victory was, however, not so great when they assembled once more, though the interest apparently was as keen as at the beginning. For some unaccountable reason the dispatches were delayed and a much longer interval than usual intervened before the welcome yellow slip was handed to the announcer. Murmurs of disappointment were heard on every side, and it became more evident with every passing moment that hope had mostly been lost. At last, however, the welcome word was received, and even Will Phelps was so eager to hear that he crowded forward into the front ranks of the assembly.

"Alden scores touchdown and goal. Winthrop fighting desperately, but outweighed and outplayed since Hawley taken out."

"It's all over but the shouting," said the sophomore whose gloomy views had been so sharply rebuked by the senior. "There isn't any use in hanging around here. Come on, fellows! Let's go where there's something a little more cheerful."

He made as if to depart from the crowd, but as no one followed him, he apparently abandoned his purpose and remained with his fellows. Only two more dispatches were read, the second of which announced the end of the game with the score still standing in favor of Alden thirteen to nothing.

"Rotten!" exclaimed the sophomore angrily. "Just what we might—" He stopped abruptly as the senior advanced to a place where he could be seen by all and began to harangue the assembly.

"Now, fellows," he began, "the best test of our spirit is that we can stand up and take this in the right way. Of course, we wanted the game, and some of us hoped and expected we would have it too. But the other team, and doubtless the better one, has won. Next year we'll be ready for them again, or rather you will, for I sha'n't be here, and the time to begin to win then is right here and now. But I want to put in a good word for our team. I haven't a doubt that they did their level best, and if we could see them now, we'd be almost as proud of them as if they had won. I know every man put in his best work. And what I propose is that we go down to the station to-night and meet them with as hearty a cheer as if they had won the game, for we know they did their best to uphold the honor of old Winthrop to a man!"

A cheer greeted the senior's words, and at ten o'clock that evening all the students who were in town assembled at the little station to greet the returning members of the team. But Will Phelps, when the train came to a standstill and the boys leaped out upon the platform, speedily forgot all about the game in the sight which greeted his eyes.

CHAPTER XVII

PETER JOHN'S DOWNFALL

In the midst of the cheering and shouting that greeted the return of the team and its supporters, Will Phelps attained a glimpse of the sturdy heroes themselves who had fought the battle of the gridiron. Some of them were somewhat battered and he could see that Hawley carried his arm in a sling. His classmate's face was pale, but as he was surrounded by a crowd of students, Will found it was impossible to make his way to him and soon gave up the attempt. He was standing somewhat back from the train eagerly watching all that was going on about him, but only in a half-hearted way joining in the excitement, for the defeat of the team and his own disappointment in not being able to make the trip had chilled his enthusiasm.

Suddenly he caught sight of Foster as he stepped down upon the platform and instantly Will began to push his way forward to greet him. As Foster stepped down he turned back as if to assist some one, and Will perceived that it was Peter John Schenck who was being assisted. But his actions were strange and his general appearance was woebegone in the extreme.

"What's the matter with Peter John? Sick?" inquired Will as he pressed forward.

"Sick? Sick nothing!" retorted Foster in a low voice. "Can't you see what ails him? The fool!"

The maudlin expression on Peter John's face, his wabbling steps, the silly smile with which he greeted Will at once disclosed what his condition was and with a feeling of disgust Will turned away.

"Hold on, Will," called Peter John tremulously, beginning to cry as he spoke, "don't go backsh on a fellow now. I los' all my money. Seven dollar I put up on the team an' they jis' sold out," and Peter John's tears increased and he threatened to fall on Foster's shoulder.

Will had turned back sharply at the words, his disgust and anger so plainly stamped upon his face that even Peter John was moved by it and began to sob audibly. "Sold out, Will! Seven dollar all gone! Too bad! Too bad!"

"Get a taxi, Will," said Foster in a low voice. "If we can get the fellow up to his room without attracting too much attention we may be able to put him in bed."

As Will turned away, he was rejoiced to notice that his classmate's condition had apparently not attracted the attention of the crowd, which was too much occupied in the excitement of greeting the team to be mindful of other matters. Disgust and anger were so mingled in Will's feelings that he was hardly aware of what he was doing, but at last he succeeded in getting a taxi, and bidding the driver hold it near the end of the platform, he hastened back to the assistance of Foster.

As he returned he noticed that Mott was now with Peter John, and only one glance was required to show that he was in a condition similar to that of Peter John, though not quite so helpless.

"Glad t' see you, freshman," stammered Mott as Will approached. "Great sport, that fellow," and he pointed stupidly at Peter John as he spoke. "Put up his monish like li'le man. No squeal from him, no, not a squeal. No, goo' man. Goo' man, freshman."

"Shall we take him too?" inquired Will of Foster.

"Yes, if there's room."

"I think there will be."

"He can make his way all right, I think, but you'll have to help me with Peter John. Get hold of his other arm. That's right," he added as Will grasped his maudlin classmate by the left arm, while Foster supported him by the right.

"Come on, Mott, if you want to ride up," said Will sharply to the sophomore.

"That ish good o' you, freshman," drawled Mott. "Broke, dead broke! Do ash much for you some day. You get broke some daysh, I s'pose."

"Shut up, Mott," said Foster savagely.

"A'-a' right. Just's you say, not's I care."

A few in the assemblage noted the condition of the boys and laughed thoughtlessly, but neither Will nor his room-mate was in a frame of mind to respond. Disgusted, angry, mortified beyond expression, they nevertheless assisted the boys to the seats in the taxi which Will had secured, and quickly doing as he was bidden, the driver started rapidly up the street. Peter John had fallen heavily against Will's shoulder and was instantly asleep, but Mott was not to be so easily disposed of. Peering out from the window at the crowds that were moving up the street and by which the taxi was passing, he emitted three or four wild whoops and then began to sing:

"We're coming, we're coming, our brave little band,On the right side of temperance we always do stand;We don't use tobacco, for this we do think,That those who do use it most always do drink."

"Mott, if you don't keep quiet I'll throw you out," exclaimed Will mortified as he perceived that the passing crowd was turning about to discover what the noisy commotion meant.

"A'-a' right," responded Mott in a shout that could have been heard far away. "I'll be as sthill as an intensified hippopotamus! Not a sound of my voice shall awake the echoes of these purple hills. I'll not be the one to arouse the slumbers of this peaceful vale."

"Driver," interrupted Will sharply, "stop your cab."

"No, no, Will, you'll only make a bad matter worse. Let's keep on and do the best we can. It'll only call attention to ourselves," said Foster hastily.

"Thatsh sho," assented Mott noisily, swaying in his seat as he spoke. "Keep on, driver. Go straight up to prexy's house; I've got something p'ticular to shay t' him. Shame, way the team sold out t'-day! Disgrace to old Winthrop! Have a good mind to leave the college myself an' go to Alden; they're men there! They know how to stan' up an' take their med'cine. Great place, Alden! Guess they'll be shorry here when they shee me with a great big A on my sweater!""Mott, keep still," exclaimed Foster.

"Keep still yerself, freshman. Don't talk t' me."

There was nothing to be done except to endure it all in silence or put the noisy student out of the taxi. Poor Will felt that the people they were passing looked upon all four of the occupants of the cab as if they were all in the same disgraceful condition. His eyes blazed and his cheeks were crimson. To him it seemed as if the cab was scarcely moving on its way to Leland Hall. The way was interminable, the suffering almost too great to be endured.

At last, however, the driver stopped before the dormitory where Mott had his room and Foster said, "Will, I'll look after this fellow if you'll attend to Peter John."

"Nobody—no freshman in p'ticular—ish going to help me!" exclaimed Mott noisily. "I can walk a chalk line, I can. Keep your eyes on me and you'll see how it's done."

"All right. Get out, then," said Foster hastily.

Mott lurched out of the cab, and the driver, at Foster's word, at once started on and neither of the boys glanced behind to see how it fared with the intoxicated sophomore. They were eager now to dispose of their classmate, and as soon as the taxi halted in front of Leland Hall they tried to arouse the slumbering freshman. At last, by dint of their united efforts, they succeeded in lifting him to the ground, and then they somehow got him up the stairway and soon had him in his bed. When their labors were ended Will exclaimed, "It must be midnight. Surely the people couldn't see who we were except when the cab passed the street lights, but I'm afraid some of them knew then."

"That isn't so bad. I don't care half so much about their seeing as I do about something else."

"What's that?"

"What they saw. Poor fool!" he added bitterly as he turned and glanced at the bed whereon Peter John was lying and noisily sleeping. "I did my best to hold him back, but he would go on with Mott."

"Do you think he lost his money too?"

"Haven't a doubt of it."

"And he didn't have very much to lose."

"It was all he had. It would have been the same if it had been seven thousand instead of just plain seven. He was so set up by the attentions of Mott that he was an easy mark. I never saw anything like it."

"Well, all I can say is that I hope I sha'n't again, but probably I shall if he stays in college," said Will bitterly.

"It's in him, that's about all one can say," said Foster. "If it hadn't been here it would have been somewhere else. And yet they say that a college is a dangerous place for a young fellow to be in."

"I don't believe it."

"No more do I. There are all kinds here the same as there are pretty much everywhere, and all there is of it is that a fellow has a little more freedom to follow out just what he wants to do."

"Come on," suggested Will, starting toward the door. "We can't do anything more for Peter John. He'll probably be around to see us to-morrow."

As the boys approached the doorway they met Hawley and at his urgent request turned back into the room with him. The big freshman glanced at his sleeping room-mate and then laughed as he said, "Too young. Ought not to have left his mother yet." As neither of the boys replied, Hawley continued, "He'll have to quit that or he'll queer himself in the college. I don't know that he can do that any more successfully than he has done already though," he added.

Will was irritated that Hawley should take the matter in such a light way and said half-angrily, "Do you suppose he'll be hauled up before the faculty?"

"Not unless they hear of it," laughed Hawley, "and I don't believe they will."

"Tell us about the game," interrupted Foster.

"My story is short and not very sweet," retorted Hawley grimly, glancing at his arm as he spoke.

"How did that happen?"

"Nobody knows. It's done and that's all there is to it. I'm out of the game for the rest of this season."

"That's too bad. Did Alden really have such a tremendous team?"

"Look at the score. You know what that was, don't you?"

"Yes, I heard. Come on, Will. We'd better be in bed. We'll get Hawley to tell us all about the game some other time. Come on."

The two freshmen at once departed, but when they were in their own room it was not the lost game which was uppermost in their minds and conversation, but the fall of Peter John. And when at last they sought their beds it was with the conviction that Peter John himself would seek them out within a day or two and try to explain how it was that his downfall had occurred. This, they thought, would give them the opportunity they desired, and if the faculty did not discover the matter and take action of their own then they might be able to say or do something to recall Peter John to himself.

On the following day, however, their classmate did not appear, and in the days that followed he did not once come to their room. Mott they had seen, but he had only laughed lightly when he met them and made no reference to the ride he had taken in their taxi.

"I don't believe Peter John knows that we know anything about what happened on his trip," said Foster thoughtfully one day.

"What makes him keep away from us all the time, then?"

"That's so. Probably his conscience isn't in the best of condition. You don't suppose he's waiting for us to make the first move, do you?"

"I don't know."

"I hate to leave the fellow to himself," said Foster. "He'll go to the dogs as sure as you're born if he is."

"If he isn't there already."

"Well, if he's there we must help to get him out."

"You're the one to do it, Foster. You aren't working up your Greek."

Will had been working with even greater intensity than before and was beginning to see the results of his labors. With his disposition there was no comparative degree. Everything was at one extreme or the other and now he was giving himself but little rest and even Peter John's disgrace was not so keenly felt by him as at the time when it had occurred.

"I think I'll have to do something," assented Foster, "or at least try to."

But on the following day an excitement broke out among the students at Winthrop that speedily and completely banished from the minds of Will and Foster even their well-intended efforts to aid their weak and misguided classmate.

CHAPTER XVIII

AN ALARMING REPORT

The excitement first came to Will Phelps when one night he was returning to his room from his dinner in the fraternity house. The house, together with four or five other similar houses, was situated in the same street with the dormitory, but was distant a walk of seven or eight minutes, and there was usually a crowd of the college boys to be seen on the village street three times a day when they passed to or from their boarding places.

On this particular evening Will chanced to be alone, and as he went on he perceived Mott approaching. He had had but little to say to the fellow since the escapade, and now as he recognized the sophomore his feeling of anger or disgust arose once more, and he was inclined to pass him with only a light nod of recognition.

But Mott was not to be so lightly turned aside or ignored, and as he saw Will he stopped, and his manner at once betrayed the excitement under which he was laboring.

"Have you heard the news, Phelps?" he demanded.

"I haven't heard anything," replied Will coldly.

"You haven't? Well, you ought to. It's all over college now."

"What's all over college?"

"Why, the report of the typhoid."

"What?" demanded Will, instantly aroused.

"I mean what I say. And there are all sorts of reports about what's to be done. Some say the faculty have decided to shut up shop for a few weeks, and some say they've sent for experts, and I don't know what all."

"Who are the fellows that are down with it?"

"Schenck—"

"Peter John?" demanded Will sharply.

"Yes, and there are seven others. He's the only freshman; there are two sophs, two juniors, and one senior. Wagner is the senior."

"Where are they?"

"They're all in the infirmary, and the whole shop has been quarantined."

"When was it found out?"

"Only to-day, this afternoon, I think. You see all eight have been under the weather for a while, and the doctor here thought it was first one thing that ailed them and then another. Last night or this morning they had a consultation, and decided that every one of the eight had typhoid fever. It's a great go, isn't it?"

"And you say Peter John is one?"

"Sure."

"Is he in the infirmary?"

"Yes, every one of them is there."

"Is he very much sick?"

"Can't tell yet, but he's sick enough."

"Can anybody see him?" inquired Will thoughtfully.

"No. There isn't any one allowed in the building except the nurses, doctors, and the families of the fellows, that is, when they come. I understand that word has been sent to all the families, and nurses have already been engaged, and that some of them are on the ground now."

"It's terrible!" said Will with a shudder.

"I know what I'm going to do," said Mott glibly.

"What's that?"

"I'm going home. Of course, the governor won't believe me at first when I tell him why I've returned to the ancestral abode, but you may rest easy when he sees it in the papers, then he'll believe it all right enough. Fine to have your daddy believe a lying newspaper before he takes the word of his own offspring, isn't it?"

"May not be all his fault."

"Yes, it is. I'd have been as decent a fellow as you or any fellow in college if I'd been treated halfway decently. But I wasn't."

Will had his own ideas as to that, but he did not express them, for the full sense of the calamity of the college was now strongly upon him. Even the shadows of the great hills seemed to him to be more sombre than usual, and in whichever direction he looked there was an outer gloom corresponding to the one within. In the first shock of the report a nameless fear swept over him, and already he was positive that in his own case he could discover certain symptoms that were the forerunners of the dreaded disease. He hastily bade Mott good-night and ran all the way back to his room.

Foster was already there, and at once he exclaimed:

"Foster, have you heard about it?"

"The typhoid?""Yes. They say Peter John and Wagner and six others are down with it."

"It's true."

"What's going to be done?"

"You mean what the college is going to do or what we're to do?"

"Yes, that's it. Both."

"I've telephoned home," said Foster quietly.

"You have?"

"Yes. I have just come back from the office."

"Did you telephone my father?"

"No. I telephoned my father and told him to ring up your house."

"And did he?"

"Of course he did."

"Did you hear anything—I mean—"

"Now, look here, Will," said Foster quietly. "Don't get rattled. I know it's bad, but there isn't any use in losing your head over it. I've been down to see the dean and have talked it over with him."

"What did he have to say?"

"He said the report was true and the eight fellows were all down with the typhoid, and that every one of them had been taken to the infirmary."

"What else?" demanded Will, his excitement increasing in spite of his effort to be calm.

"That's what I'm trying to tell you, if you'll give me half a chance. He said the president had sent for the best experts in the country, and that everything that it was possible to do would be done. He said too, that they would deal absolutely squarely with the boys, and if it was discovered that there was the least danger of it spreading they would tell us, and if necessary they'd close for a while till the whole thing had been ferreted out."

"That's square."

"Of course it is."

"What are you going to do, Foster?"

"Nothing, that is, for a day or two anyway. I've told my father, and if he thinks I'd better come home he'll say so."

"But he may not know."

"He will in a day or two."

"What are you going to do now?"

"Study my Greek."

"I ought to, but I'm going out for a little while. I've got to cool off a bit before I can settle down to work."

"Don't be gone long. You'll only see the fellows and get stirred up all the more. I'd drop it and go to 'boning.' It's the best cure."

"It is for a fellow like you, Foster. I can't do it yet. I've got to get outdoors till I can get my breath again."

Seizing his cap Will went out into the night. He passed by Leland Hall and glancing up discovered that there was a light in Peter John's room. Instantly he entered the building and bounding up the stairway knocked on his classmate's door, and in response to the invitation entered and found Hawley within and alone.

"Hello, Hawley. What's the news about Peter John?"

"Oh, he's got it. Temperature a hundred and four and a half and all that sort of thing."

"Any idea where or how he got it?""Not the least."

"Have you seen him?"

"Since he went to the infirmary? Yes, once; but I sha'n't see him again till he comes out well or—"

"Is he the worst?"

"No. Wagner seems to be the hardest hit, but they told me you couldn't tell very much about it yet. Have to wait a few days anyway."

"Mott says he is going home."

"Yes, there probably will be a lot of the fellows leaving by to-morrow."

"Are you afraid?"

"Some."

"Going to leave?"

"I'm going to wait a day or two and see what turns up before I decide just what I shall do."

On his way back to his room Will fell in with several others of his classmates, and the exciting conversation was repeated in each case until at last when he joined Foster, whom he found still poring over his lesson in Greek for the morrow, his feelings were so overwrought that he was almost beside himself.

"Everybody's going to leave, Foster," he declared.

"Not quite, for I'm not going yet myself."

"But—" Will ceased abruptly as he perceived that a messenger boy was standing in front of his door. Quickly seizing the envelope he perceived that it was directed to himself and instantly tearing it open he read:

"If new cases develop within three days come home. Otherwise remain. Wire me daily." The message was signed by his father.

"That settles it!" exclaimed Will, "I'm going to bed. Splinter will be easy on us to-morrow anyway."

Foster smiled as he shook his head and continued his own work, but his room-mate was not aware of either action.

In chapel on the following morning the president of the college reiterated the statement which the dean already had made to Foster, and after trying to show the students that a panic was even more to be feared than the fever, and promising to keep them fully and frankly informed as to the exact status of affairs, he dismissed them to their recitations, which it was understood were to be continued without interruption, at least for the present.

In his Greek that day Will failed miserably and completely, and his anger at Splinter was intensified when the professor near the close of the recitation said:

"It is quite needless, I fawncy, for me to emphasize, young gentlemen, the necessity there is at the present time for you all to adopt the utmost care in all matters pertaining especially to your health. I refer to you individually as well as collectively. My advice to you is to use only mineral water—I refer obviously to the water you drink—and it might be well to avoid the undue use of milk—"

A shout of laughter interrupted the professor which caused his face to flush with anger and he arose abruptly from his seat, the signal that the class was dismissed.

As Will, who was among the last to pass out, came near the desk the professor said to him, "Mr. Phelps, I should be pleased if you would remain for a brief time. I should like exceedingly to have a word with you."

Accordingly, Will stood by the desk till all the class had passed out, and then the professor said, "Ah, Mr. Phelps, would you kindly inform me what your opinion is as to the cause of the students receiving my remarks a few minutes ago with such an outburst of laughter? I assure you I had not the least intention to say anything that should even appear to be liable to excite the mirth of the young gentlemen. I do not know that I was ever more serious in my entire life."

"I think, professor, it was your reference to milk."

"Why should I not refer to it? In times of fear, when typhoid fever is—is—ah, at least somewhat feared, it is wise to be extremely cautious, and I have it on the authority of men of the highest reputation that milk is a medium through which the germs of the disease transmit themselves most readily."

"Yes, but you know, professor, the college is supposed to think the freshmen feed on milk. That's supposed to be their diet."

"Ah, yes," replied the professor, smiling in a manner that proclaimed his entire inability to perceive the point. "That must be the point of the joke. Ah, yes. I see it distinctly now. It is very good! It is very good, indeed!"

"Professor, can you tell me my marks? How am I doing in my Greek lately?"

"I am not supposed to reply to such a question from any of the young gentlemen, but I fawncy in a general way I may be able to respond to your query. Ah, yes," he added, glancing at the page in the little book before him wherein Will's record was contained, "there is an improvement, not great, it is true, but still an improvement; and if your work continues it will bring you almost up to the mark required."

"Almost?" exclaimed Will aghast. "You don't mean to say, do you, Mr. Splinter—
"

"Mr. who?" demanded the professor, instantly rising and his face flushing again with anger.

CHAPTER XIX

A RARE INTERVIEW

Instantly Will Phelps was overwhelmed with confusion. His face flushed crimson and his knees shook under the excitement which quickly seized upon him. The opprobrious title by which the Greek professor was known among the students and by which he was commonly spoken of by them had slipped from his tongue almost unconsciously. He stood staring stupidly into the professor's face, while visions of expulsion and future difficulty flashed into his troubled mind.

"I beg your pardon, professor," he managed to ejaculate at last. "I did not mean to say that. The word slipped out before I knew it. I am very sorry for it, for I certainly did not intend to be disrespectful in any way."

"You insulted me!" exclaimed the professor in a rage that under other circumstances would have seemed almost ludicrous to Will. It was like the anger of an infuriated canary bird or of some little child.

"Then I want to apologize," said Will quietly. "As I said, I certainly did not intend to do anything of the kind."

"But you did," persisted the outraged teacher. "You most assuredly did."

"Can't you believe me when I say it was not intentional?"

"That does not excuse it, but I fawncy the tendency among the young gentlemen of the college is to bestow appellations upon the various members of the faculty that are not warranted."

"I have heard some of them spoken of in that way, but I don't think the fellows meant either to be disrespectful or unkind," said Will eagerly.

"No, I fawncy it may in part be due to the thoughtlessness of youth and I would not be unduly harsh with you after your ample apology. Then you have been accustomed to hear me myself referred to as Splinter, have you?"

"I—yes—that is—" stammered Will.

"Precisely. Now what in your opinion is the basis upon which the students have added such a derisive epithet to my name?"

Will was silent, though in spite of his efforts the expression of his face betrayed somewhat the feeling of blank amazement which possessed him.

"I fawncy I can trace its derivation," said the professor simply. "Doubtless when I first became a member of the faculty the appellation, or, let me see, is it an appellation or a cognomen, as you commonly have heard it?"

"Yes, sir," Will managed to respond.

"It is, then, as I fawncied, and doubtless was bestowed upon me as indicative of my lack of avoirdupois. And it was not entirely unnatural that they should do so, for at the time when I came to Winthrop I was very slight, very slight indeed. The appellation, or cognomen, was without doubt given in recognition of that fact, a custom not unknown, among the classical nations and one prevalent among the Hebrews and even among the Indians of America. The history of names would provide an exceedingly interesting field of study for you, Mr. Phelps."

Will bowed but did not speak, for he was afraid to interrupt or to divert the childlike man from the channel in which his thoughts appeared to be running.

"Such a name once given," resumed the professor, "would doubtless cling to one long after physical changes had been made that would no longer afford an accurate basis for the nomenclature. But I was very slight, very slight indeed, Mr. Phelps, when I first came here some seventeen years ago, or, to be exact, seventeen years and four months, that is, four months lacking a few days. Why, I believe I weighed only one hundred and seventeen pounds at the time."

Will strove to be duly impressed by the fact, but as he looked at the man who was somewhat above six feet in height and whose body did not give many tokens of having increased materially in breadth or thickness since the time to which the professor referred, he found it extremely difficult to repress the smile that rose to his lips.

"Yes," resumed the professor quickly, "I have increased in weight since that time but the appellation still clings and doubtless will as long as I remain in Winthrop."

"How much do you weigh now, professor?" The moment Will asked the question he regretted it, but the temptation was too strong to be resisted.

"I cannot say exactly," said the professor in some confusion, "but my weight has very materially increased. If I recall aright, the last time when I was weighed I had added two and three-quarters pounds. It is true it was in the winter and doubtless heavier clothing may have slightly modified the result. But still I can safely affirm that I am much heavier than I was at the time when I joined the Winthrop faculty."

"Do you find that you feel better now that you are more corpulent? I have heard it said that addition to the body is subtraction from the brain. Do you think that is so, professor?"

"It is true, most assuredly. All classifical literature confirms the statement you have just made."

"Then you don't believe in athletics, do you, professor?"

"Assuredly not. Most assuredly not."

"But didn't the ancient Greeks have their racecourses? Didn't they believe in running and jumping and boxing and I don't know what all?"

"That is true, but the times were very different then. They had not in the least lost the sense of the poetry of life. They were not so crassly or grossly materialistic as the present age undoubtedly is. Every grove was peopled with divinities, every mountain was the abode of the unseen. Why, Mr. Phelps, the Greeks were the only people that ever lived that looked upon mountains as anything but blots or defects."

"Is that so?" inquired Will in surprise.

"It certainly is. It is true that since the days of the poet Gray there has been a tendency among English-speaking people to affect a veneration for the mountains, but it is, I fawncy, only a faint echo of the old Greek conception and is a purely superficial product of an extremely superficial age and people.""Didn't the Hebrews have a feeling like the one you tell of? Isn't there a psalm that begins 'I will lift up mine eyes unto the hills, from whence cometh my help'? Didn't they describe the high hills that were round about Jerusalem?"

"Ah, yes. That is true," assented the professor in some confusion. "I had not thought of it in that light precisely. You have given me a new insight to-day,

Mr. Phelps. I shall at once go over my data again. I am grateful to you for acceding to my request to remain to-day."

"But, professor," persisted Will, "what about my work in Greek? I've had a tutor ever since you told me to get one and I've been working hard too. Today I didn't do very well, but I was so excited about the fever, for Peter John—I mean Schenck—is one of the fellows to come down with it, you know, and we've been telephoning and telegraphing home—"

"Ah, yes. But you heard my remarks to-day concerning the necessity of increased work in Greek as a preventive, did you not?"

"I did. But, professor, I'm willing to work. If I'm to be shut out of the exam—I mean the examination—as you seem to think I will, anyway, I don't see any use in my trying any more."

The expression on the professor's face became instantly harder as he said, "I fawncy the effort to curry favor with the various members of the faculty is not very popular with the student body."

"Do you think I'm trying to 'boot-lick'?" demanded Will quickly.

"I look upon that term as somewhat objectionable, but I fawncy in the vernacular of college life it is one that is quite expressive."

"I'm not trying to boot-lick you or any other professor!" retorted Will, now feeling angry and insulted as well. "I didn't stay here to-day because I wanted to. You yourself asked me to do it. And I asked you a perfectly fair question. I knew I hadn't been doing very well, but after I saw you I've been trying, honestly trying, to do better. And all the encouragement you give me is to say that if I work harder I may almost come up to the passing mark."

"Pardon me, Mr. Phelps, but you are the one to change your record, not I. All I do is merely to jot down what you have been doing. I do not do the work—I merely record it."

For a moment Will Phelps was almost speechless with anger. He felt outraged and insulted in every fibre of his being. He hastily bade the professor good-morning, and, seizing his cap, rushed for his room, a great fear being upon him that unless he instantly departed he would say or do something for which he would have a lifelong regret.

As he burst into his room he found Foster already there, and, flinging his books savagely across the room, Will seated himself in his easy-chair and glared at his room-mate.

"Why? What's wrong? What's happened, Will?" demanded Foster, in astonishment.

"Oh, I've just had another delightful interview with old Splinter. He's the worst I ever struck yet!"

"Did you strike him, Will?" inquired Foster, a smile of amusement appearing on his face.

"No, but I'd like to! His soul would get lost in the eye of a needle! He's the smallest specimen I have ever run up against. He may know Greek, but he doesn't know anything else. I never in all my life saw—"

"Tell me about it, Will," interrupted Foster.

Thus bidden, Will related the story of his interview with his professor of Greek. When Foster laughed as he told of Splinter's description of his marvelously increased corpulence, Will did not join, for the ludicrous side now was all swallowed up in his anger. And when his room-mate scowled as he heard of the professor's insinuation that the young freshman was trying to "boot-lick," Will's anger broke forth afresh. "What's the use in my trying, I'd like to know?" he demanded. "I've never tried harder in my life than I have for the last three or four weeks. And what does old Splinter have to say about it? 'Oh, I'm doing better and if I keep on I'll almost come up to the passing mark!' I tell you, it isn't fair! It isn't right! He's just determined to put me out!"

"Perhaps he thinks he's bound to stick to the marks he's given you before."

"Yes, that's it. But think of it, Foster. Here I am doing better and putting in my best work. And the old fellow acknowledges it too, for he says so himself. But what does it all amount to? He doesn't give me any credit for what I've been doing lately. No, he's just tied up to the marks I got at the beginning of the year. What fairness is there in that, I'd like to know? That's the way they do in State's prison, but I didn't suppose old Winthrop was built exactly on that plan. I thought the great point here was to wake a man up and inspire him to try to do better and all that sort of thing. And I am doing better, and I know it, and so does he, but his soul is so dried up and withered that he can't think of anything but ancient history. He hasn't the least idea of what's going on here to-day. I'll bet the old fellow, when he has the toothache, groans in dactylic hexameters and calls for his breakfast in the Ionic dialect. Bah! What's all the stuff good for anyway? I haven't any reason for trying any more."

"Yes, you have."

"I have? Well, what is it?"

"Your father, if nothing else."

Will instantly became silent, for Foster's words only seemed to call up before him the vision of his father's face. He was the best man that had ever lived, Will declared to himself, and his conviction had been strengthened as he had seen the relations between many of his college mates and their fathers. How he would be grieved over it all. And yet Will knew that never an unkind word would be spoken. It was almost more than he could bear, he thought, and his eyes were glistening when he arose from his seat to respond to a knock on the door. As he opened it he saw standing before him his own father and the father of Peter John Schenck, and with a yell of delight he grasped his father's outstretched hand and pulled him hastily into the room.

CHAPTER XX

A CRISIS

In response to Will's eager questions, Mr. Phelps explained that he had come to Winthrop to satisfy himself as to the exact status as to the fever that had broken out. Before he had come up to Will's room he had consulted the college officials and now felt that he was in a position to decide calmly what must be done by his son.

"And what's the verdict?" inquired Will.

"It will not be necessary for you to return. I think everything is being done that ought to be and though we shall be anxious, still I am not unduly alarmed. I have confidence in you, Will, and I am sure you will not be careless in a time like this. The president informs me that there have not been any new cases since the first outbreak, and he is of the opinion that all these cases were due to one cause and that was found outside of the village."

"Then you don't want me to go home with you?" inquired Will quizzically.

"What I might 'want' and what is best are two different matters," said his father with a smile, "Just at present what I want and what you need happen to be one and the same thing."

"What's that?"

"Your Greek."

Will's face clouded and then unmindful of the others who were in the room he told his father of his recent interview with his professor of Greek. The smile of amusement on the face of Mr. Phelps when Will began soon gave way to an expression of deep concern. To Will, who understood him so thoroughly, it was evident that his father was angry as well as disappointed, and for a moment there was a feeling of exultation in his own heart. Now something would be done, he felt confident, and the injustice under which he was laboring and suffering would be done away.

"Your other work is all right, Will?" inquired his father after a brief silence.

"Oh, yes! Fine! If old Splinter was only half the man that Professor Sinclair is, there wouldn't be a bit of trouble. Why the recitation in Latin never seems to be more than fifteen minutes long. But the Greek—bah! The hour is like a week of Sundays!"

"Still, Will, there is only one way out of it for you."

"I suppose so," responded Will, his heart sinking as he spoke.

"Yes, it must be faced. I know it's hard, but you can't get around it, Will, and I'm sure you don't want to run from it. As I told you, it isn't as if your Greek professor was the only one of his kind you will meet in life, for his name is legion and you will find him everywhere. The only thing for you to do is to keep on with your tutor and prove yourself to be the master. If you do that, the experience, hard as it is, may prove to be one of the best that could come to you."

Will was silent for a moment before he spoke, and then he said impulsively, "Well, pop, I suppose you are right. I'll do my best.""Of course you will," responded his father quietly, though his eyes were shining. "It isn't so hard for you as it is for Mr. Schenck."

"Is Peter John worse?" inquired Will quickly.

"Yes."

"Isn't there something we can do?" said Will eagerly.

"No, nothing," said Mr. Schenck. "My boy is very sick, but all we can do is to wait. He is having good care. The only comfort I have is what they tell me about him and what he has been doing since he came to college."

Both boys looked up quickly, but neither spoke and Mr. Schenck continued. "Yes, there's a young man I have met since I've been here who has told me many things about my boy that comfort me now very much."

"Was it Mott?" interrupted Will.

"Yes, that was his name. You know him too, I see. He seems to be a very fine young man. He told me that Peter was one of the leaders in his class, and that everybody in the college knew him. He said too, that he had won his numerals—though I don't just understand what that means."

"It means that he has the right to wear the number of his class on his cap or sweater," said Will. "That's more than I've won." He had not the heart to undeceive the unhappy man, though both he and Foster were aware that Mott had been overstating the facts in his desire to comfort Peter John's father.

"Well, I hope he'll get well," said Mr. Schenck with a heavy sigh, "though it does seem as if such things always happened to the brightest boys. I'm going to stay here for a few days till I know he's better or—" The sentence was not completed and for a time there was a tense silence in the room.

At last the men departed, Mr. Schenck to go to his son's room where he was to sleep while he remained in Winthrop, and Mr. Phelps to the station where he was to take the train for his home. Will accompanied his father, but the subject that was uppermost in the mind of each was not referred to for there are times when silence is golden.

In the days that followed, Will Phelps worked as he never had worked before in all his brief life. His distaste for the Greek and dislike of the professor were as strong as before, and at times it almost seemed to him that he could no longer continue the struggle. His sole inspiration was in the thought of his father and in his blind determination not to be mastered.

An additional element of gloom in those days were the reports that came from the infirmary of the condition of Peter John. All the other patients appeared to be doing well, but the daily word from the watchers by Peter John's bedside was that he was worse. A pall seemed to be resting over the entire college. The noisy songs and boisterous shouts were not heard in the dormitories nor upon the campus.

A part of the general anxiety was gone when as the days passed there were no reports of new cases developed, but the fear of what was to be the issue in the case of Peter John was in every heart—even with those who had not exchanged a word with him since he had entered Winthrop.

Will Phelps found himself even wondering how it was that the "old grads" when they returned always spoke in such enthusiastic terms of their own college days. How they laughed and slapped one another on the back as they recalled and recounted their exploits. It was Will's conviction that those days must have been markedly different from those through which he was passing, for he was finding only hard work and much trouble, he dolefully assured himself. He was too inexperienced to understand that one is never able to see clearly the exact condition of present experiences. There is then no perspective, and the good and evil, the large and small, are strangely confused. It is like the figures in a

Chinese picture wherein the background and foreground, the little and the big, are much the same in their proportions. Only when a man looks back and beholds the events of the bygone days in their true perspective is he able to form a correct estimate of the relative values. Even Will Phelps would not have believed that there might come a day when the very struggle he was having in mastering his Greek would be looked upon by him as not unpleasant in the larger light in which all his college days would be viewed.

Mr. Schenck still remained in Winthrop, and his face every morning when Will went to inquire about Peter John was a sure indication of the report which was to be made even before a word had been spoken. Steadily lower and lower sank the freshman, who was desperately ill, until at last the crisis came, and with the passing of the day the issue of life or death would be determined.

In the interval between his recitations Will ran to see the suffering man and learn how the issue was going, and when at last the word was received that Peter John, if no relapse occurred, was likely to recover, he felt as if a great load had been lifted from his mind. It was his first experience with the deep tragedy that, like a cloud, rests over all mankind, and in the glimmer of hope that now appeared it seemed to him that all things appeared in a new light. Even his detested Greek was not quite so bad as it previously had been, and in the reaction that came Will bent to his distasteful task with a renewed determination.

When several weeks had elapsed, and the time of the Christmas vacation was near, for the first time Will was permitted to enter the room where Peter John was sitting up in bed. It was difficult for Will to hide the shock that came when he first saw his classmate, his face wasted till it almost seemed as if the bones must protrude, his head shaved, and his general weakness so apparent as to be pathetic.

Striving to conceal his real feelings and to appear bright and cheery, Will extended his hand and said nervously: "I'm mighty glad to see you, Peter John, and so will all the fellows be. I don't think you've taken the best way of getting a vacation."

Peter John smiled in a way that almost brought the tears to Will's eyes, and said, "I'm much obliged to you, Will."

"No, you're not. We're all much obliged to you for getting well. I don't know what the track team would have done without you."

"Guess I won't bother the track team this year. That's what the doctor says.""Oh, well," said Will hastily, "that won't make any difference. You'll be all right for another year and that will do just as well."

"Say, Will," said Peter after a brief pause:

"What is it?" inquired Will kindly.

"There's something I want to say to you."

"Say it, then," laughed Will.

"I'm never going to touch a drop again."

"That's all right. Of course you won't," assented Will cordially.

"And, Will—"

"Yes?"

"I'm not going to have anything charged up to you any more."

"'Anything charged up to me'? I don't know what you mean."

"I mean those cakes and pies I had charged to you down at Tommie's." "Tommie" was the name by which the proprietor of one of the little restaurants and bakeshops in Winthrop was familiarly called by the college boys.

"I didn't know you had anything charged to me."

"You didn't?"

"No. I haven't had any bill for it, anyway."

"You'll get it. You'll have one," said Peter John nodding his head decidedly. "I don't know what I ever did it for anyway. At first I thought it was a good joke on you. M—some of the fellows said it would be. And then somehow I kept it up."

"Never mind, Peter John. I'll fix it. It'll be all right."

"Did you tell my father?" inquired Peter John anxiously."No. I haven't told him anything."

"I'm glad. I lost some money on that trip with the football team, Will."

"How much?"

"Seven dollars and a half. It was all I'd got."

"Do you want—" Will started to take out his pocketbook, but stopped abruptly, for he was not certain just how Peter John might receive his offer. He did not see the light that came for a moment into his classmate's eyes or the look of disappointment that quickly followed it.

"I'm never going to bet any more," remarked Peter John simply.

"Of course not."

"But my money is gone and I sha'n't be able to pay for those things I had charged to you at Tommie's, as I fully meant to."

"Never mind that."

"I'm going to study harder too."

"Not just yet. I shouldn't bother my head about such things now, Peter John. Wait till you are up and around before you do that."

"I'm afraid that'll be a long time."

"No. Oh no, it won't," said Will cheerily. "You'll be all right before you know it."

Peter John shook his head and was about to reply, when Mott entered the room and at the same time the physician also came. The latter glanced keenly at his patient, and then said to the visitors, "That's enough this time, boys. You'd better cut it short now and come again."

Will and Mott at once departed after bidding Peter John good-bye, and when they were out on the sidewalk Mott began to laugh.

"What's struck you? I don't see anything so very funny," said Will irritated by his companion's manner.

"Peter John has made a clean breast of it."

"What of it?"

"Oh, nothing much. Only when the 'devil was sick the devil a monk would be.' You know the words probably. It strikes me as absolutely funny."

"I don't see anything to laugh about," retorted Will warmly.

"You wait and maybe you will later, Phelps. Tra, la, freshman!" and Mott abruptly departed.

His words, however, still lingered in Will's mind, and throughout the evening the jingling rhyme that the sophomore had repeated kept running through his thoughts.

CHAPTER XXI

THE EXAMINATION

Vacation had come and gone. How Will Phelps did enjoy that break in his work! He almost begrudged the swiftly passing hours while he was at home, and as the vacation drew near its close he found himself computing the hours and even the minutes that yet remained before he must return, just as he had previously reckoned the time that must pass before he could return to Sterling. It was not that he did not enjoy his college life, for as we know he had entered heartily into its spirit, but the work was hard and his handicap in the one subject had robbed him of the enthusiasm which perhaps otherwise he might have had.

When the day at last arrived when he was to return he was unusually quiet and seldom had a word to say to any one. Uppermost in his thoughts was the expression of the principal of the school where he had prepared for college, who had said to him: "Well, Will, with all the fun of college there is still another side to it, and that is, that when a fellow enters college he really is leaving home. From that time forward he may come back for his vacations, but it is nevertheless the break that sooner or later comes to every man." Will had thought much of the saying, and its truthfulness was so apparent that he was unable entirely to shake off the somewhat depressing effect it had produced upon himself.

When the hour came and the good-byes must be said he strove desperately to be calm, but he dared not trust himself to say much. He did not once glance behind him as he walked away from the house to the street, though he knew that his father and mother were standing on the piazza and were watching him as long as his sturdy form could be seen by them.

On the train he found several of his college friends and it became somewhat easier for him in their company to forget his own heaviness of heart, and as he sped on toward Winthrop the numbers increased and the noisy shouts of greeting and the enthusiasm of the students diverted him from the feeling to which otherwise he might have yielded.

Peter John and Foster were in the number of the returning students, the former having recovered sufficiently to warrant him in taking up a part of his work. Wagner also and several of the other students who had been victims of the fever were on the train when it arrived at Winthrop, and in the warmth of their reception by their student friends there was a tonic such as even the physicians' prescriptions had not afforded. Will found a slight return of his depression when he first entered his room, but when a few days had passed his life had once more settled into the grooves of the daily routine and assumed its former round of tasks.

The mid-year examinations came within a month after the reopening of the college, and the chagrin and anger of Will Phelps were keenly aroused when he learned that although he had done well in his other studies he was conditioned in his Greek. He stormed and raved about the injustice with which he was being treated, and finally, at Foster's suggestion, sought a personal interview with his professor.

"I don't understand it, professor," he said warmly. "I never felt more sure of anything in my life than I did that I had passed that exam—I mean that examination."

"Ah, yes," replied the professor. "Quite likely if you had had the decision to make, you would have passed cum laude! Ha, ha! Yes, I fawncy it might have been so, but unfortunately the decision had to be made by other parties."

"But didn't I pass the examination, professor?" demanded Will.

"I do not exactly recollect as to that. Quite likely you failed, since that impression seems to be vivid in your thoughts. Were you so reported?"

"Yes, sir. Have you got that paper, professor?"

"I have it. I should not say I have got it."

"May I see it?" Will's manner was subdued, but there was a flush on his cheeks which those who knew him well would at once have understood.

"I will look it over with you," assented the professor. "It is against our rules to return papers to students, and I fawncy our rules are made to be obeyed, not ignored."

"Yes, sir." Will was hardly aware of what he was saying so impatient and eager was he for the paper to be produced.

The professor unlocked a drawer in his desk and drew forth a package of papers that were carefully tied with a piece of ribbon. Even the knot was exact and the loop on one side did not vary from that on the other by the smallest fraction. In his impatience Will noticed even this detail, but it was ignored in a moment when the professor slowly and with care examined the headlines of the papers and at last drew forth one which he placed on the desk in front of him and said: "Ah, yes. Here is the paper in question. It is credited with being two points above the mark required to pass a student."

"It is?" demanded Will enthusiastically. "I thought there must be a mistake."

There was a slight scowl on the professor's brow as he said: "Ah, yes. I will now refer to your true mark," and he drew forth a little book as he spoke and carefully examined the record. "Ah, yes," he murmured, not lifting his eyes from the page on which he had placed a forefinger. "Ah, yes. It is as I fawncied. Your average for the term in your recitations is what brings you below. It is true you are two above the required mark in your examination, but you are three below in your recitation work, and that, I regret exceedingly to say, brings you still one point below the mark necessary to pass you." The professor looked up and smiled blandly.

But Will Phelps was not smiling and his vigorous young heart was filled with wrath. By a desperate effort, however, he contrived to control his voice and said quietly: "Was I not doing better? Was I not improving in my work?"

"I should not care to speak positively, but my impression is that you were. Ah, yes," he added as he glanced again at his record. "You were improving. I may even say there was a marked improvement."

"And I passed the exam?"

"I have told you that you were two points above the mark required for passing the examination," said the professor with dignity.

"Then I don't see what I'm stuck for."

"You are not 'stuck'."

"I'm not? Thank you, professor. I thought I was. You can't understand what a load—"

"Excuse me, Mr. Phelps. I did not affirm that you were not conditioned. I merely declared that you were not 'stuck'."

"Then I am conditioned, am I?" said Will, his heart instantly sinking.

"Most certainly."

"What shall I have to do?"

"Pass the examination."

"But I have passed it! I passed this one!" declared Will promptly.

Again the professor's scowl returned and his thin lips were tightly compressed as he said, "I fawncy it will not be necessary for me to repeat what I have already said. You were deficient in the term work and therefore are conditioned."

"Then you mean to tell me, do you," said Will, no longer able to repress his rising indignation, "that, though I steadily improved in my class work, and then passed the examination, in spite of it all you are going to give me a condition because according to your figures I am still one point below?"

"Most certainly."

"And I'll have to take another exam?"

"Precisely."

"Good evening, professor," said Will, rising abruptly.There was nothing more to be said, and he felt that it would be wise to withdraw from the professor's presence before, in his indignation, he should say something he was certain to regret. When, however, he returned to his own room, there the flood tides of his wrath broke loose. He related the interview to Foster, and bitterly declared that if a smaller specimen of a man could be found with a microscope he thought he would be willing to spend his days and nights searching for him. There was neither justice nor fairness in it. He had improved steadily, even Splinter acknowledged that he had, and had passed the required exam, and yet for the sake of the professor's pettiness and the red tape of the college rules he must take another, and then if he should pass that he would be all right. Bah! Greek was bad enough, but Splinter was worse. What kind of a man was he to put in charge of a lot of fellows with live blood in their veins, he'd like to know. For his part he wished he was out of it. Such things might do for kids, but it was too contemptible to think of for college students.

Foster wisely waited till the outburst had been ended and then said, "Well, Will, you're up against it, whatever you say. What are you going to do about it?"

"Do about it? I'm going to pass that exam. There isn't any other way out. I've got to do it! but that doesn't make it any nicer for me, does it?"

"Splinter's here and is likely to stay. And if you and I are going to stay too, I suppose we'll have to come to his tune."

"I fancy—you should hear Splinter say that.""Say what?"

"'Fancy,' only he calls it 'fawncy'. I 'fawncy' my father is dead right when he says that I'll find a splinter everywhere and just as long as I live; but I don't believe I'll ever find one as bad as this one is."

"He may be worse. Don't you remember that little bit of Eugene Field's verse where he tells how when he was a boy he was sliding down hill with some other little chaps in front of the deacon's house? And how their yelling annoyed the deacon till at last he came out and sprinkled ashes on the path? Well, Eugene said he always had found since that there was some one standing ready to throw ashes on his path, it didn't seem to make any difference where he was."

"I don't remember, but it's like my father's words about finding splinters everywhere. Oh, no, I'm mad about it, but I'm not running away. I'm going to do it if that's the thing to be done."

And when a month had gone by Will had passed the examination, and was facing his work without the drag of work undone to hinder him.

The final influence had come one Sunday in the college chapel where the pulpit from week to week was occupied ("filled" was a word also occasionally used) by men of eminence, who were invited for the purpose of speaking to the college boys. Some of these visitors by words, presence, and message were a great inspiration to the young men, and others were correspondingly deficient, for in the vocabulary of Winthrop there was no word by which to express the comparative degree.

Will Phelps had regularly attended the services, not only because such attendance was required by the college authorities but also from the habit and inclination of his own life. With his fellows he had enjoyed some speakers and had disliked others in his thoughtless manner, and in the preceding week had laughed as heartily as any one over the unconscious escapade of Mott. The preacher for the day had been unusually prosy, having length without much breadth or thickness as Foster had dryly described the discourse, and in the midst of the hour, Mott had fallen asleep in his pew. Short and stout in figure, doubtless doubly wearied by the late hours he had kept the preceding night, in the midst of his slumbers he had begun to snore. From low and peaceful intonations he had passed on to long, prolonged, and sonorous notes that could be heard throughout the college chapel. Nor would any one of his fellows disturb his slumbers, and when at last with an unusually loud and agonizing gasp Mott was awakened and suddenly sat erect and stared stupidly about him, the good-hearted, but boyishly irreverent audience, it is safe to affirm, was decidedly more interested in the slumbering sophomore than in the soporific speaker, though few doubtless thought them related as cause and effect.

On the following Sunday Will was thinking of Mott's experience and wondering if he would give another exhibition. This thought was even in his mind when the visiting speaker entered the chapel pulpit and reverently began the service of the day.

He had not been speaking long before it was evident that every eye was fastened upon him. It was evident that here was first of all a man, and then a man who was present because he had something to say and not merely because he had to say something.

"I am appealing to those of you," he was saying, "who are eager and earnest, not to you who are indifferent or weaklings. Those of you who are members of your college teams, who are leading spirits in the college life, who are not living lives that are above reproach because you have no temptation to be bad, but because if you do right it is because you have to struggle and fight for it—it is to you I am speaking this morning."

Will was listening intently, as was every one in the chapel, and then there followed a sentence that seemed to him almost electric with life and that made a lasting impression upon his life.

CHAPTER XXII

A FRESH EXCITEMENT

"What I want every one of you young men to do," the speaker was saying, "is to give your better self a chance. There isn't one of you to-day who is not proud of his physical strength, not one of you who, if he should be urged to join one of the athletic teams, would not willingly, even proudly go through all the training that would be required of him. And that is right. In your intellectual work some of you see what the desired end is—the development of power, getting your brains into form so that you can meet and compete with the forces you will have to face when you leave your college days behind you and go forth to make your name and place in the great battlefield of life. Some of you, it may be, do not as yet see this clearly, and when you can evade a task or dodge a difficult demand upon you, count it as so much gained. But in your heart of hearts you know better, and are dimly conscious that you are losing and not gaining by your neglect."

The earnestness, the sincerity, and naturalness of the speaker acted upon Will Phelps with the effect of an electric shock. Never had he been so thoroughly aroused, and every nerve in his body was tingling when he left the chapel and started toward his own room.

"That's the kind of a talk the fellows like."

Will glanced up and beheld Wagner, who had overtaken him and now was walking by his side."I never heard such a man in all my life," said Will warmly.

"There isn't a man that comes here who has such a grip on the students as he has. One of the best things you have to look forward to is the treat you will have every year of hearing him. There isn't a spark of 'cant' or 'gush' about him, but what he says goes straight home. I don't think I'll ever forget some of the things he has said to us while I've been in college."

Accepting Will's cordial invitation, Wagner went with him to his room and remained there for an hour, and for the most of the time their conversation was of the man and the message they had that morning heard.

"I'll never forget one thing he said," remarked Wagner thoughtfully.

"What was that?" inquired Will, deeply interested at once.

"He was talking once about the reason why women were supposed to be so much more religious than men, and he said he didn't believe they were."

"There are more in the churches, anyway," suggested Will.

"Yes, that's what he said; but he said too, that the reason for it was because one side of the life of Christ had been emphasized at the expense of the other. He said so much had been made of his gentleness and meekness and the kindly virtues, which were the feminine side of his nature and appealed most to women, that he was afraid sometimes the other the stronger side and the one that appealed most to men had been lost. And then, he went on to speak of the Lion of the tribe of Judah, and he pictured the temptation and the power of decision and the heroic endurance and strength, and all that. I never heard anything like it in all my life. It made me feel as I do when the team is in for a meet. I'll never forget it! Never!"

"I wish I'd heard it."

"You'll have three more chances, anyway."

"Maybe more than that if I don't pass in all my work," laughed Will.

"Having any trouble?"

"A little with my Greek, but I've passed off my condition now."

"I think you're all right then, though Splinter is a hard proposition. Just imagine him talking like this man this morning."

Will laughed, and then becoming serious, he said, "Wagner, I've a classmate who is bothering me."

"Who is it?"

"Schenck. Peter John everybody calls him."

"What's he doing? What's the trouble with him?"

"Well, to be honest, he's drinking hard."

"Wasn't he one of the fellows who was down, with the typhoid when I had it?"

"Yes."

"An awkward, ungainly, redheaded fellow?"

"That's the one."

"What have you been doing for him?"

"Everything I could think of, but nothing seems to hold. He made all sorts of promises when he was sick and he hasn't kept one of them. He goes around with Mott and you know what that means.""Yes," said Wagner thoughtfully.

"He's a queer chap. I was in school three years with him and in some ways he was absolutely idiotic. For a while he'd work all right and then without a word of warning he'd break out and do some of the most absolutely fool things you ever heard of."

"Not very much to appeal to, I fancy."

"There might be if a fellow knew how, but I confess I don't."

"You think it would do any good for me to see him?"

"Yes, I do," said Will eagerly. "You know he might stand a show for the track team—"

"Is he the fellow that won the half-mile in the sophomore-freshman meet?" inquired Wagner eagerly. "Is he the one?"

"Yes."

"I'll see him. I'll go right over there now. You're not letting up any in your own work for the team are you, Phelps?"

"I'm doing a little all the time," Will admitted, "but I don't suppose it will amount to much."

"Yes, it will. You never can tell till you try. If Mott does not do better he'll find himself out of it. We'll need you and every one we can get. You know I can't go in this year."

"Why not?"

"The typhoid. Doctor won't let me."

"Then Peter John can't go in either."

"That's so. I hadn't thought of that. All the more reason then why you ought to do your best, Phelps. I'll see this John Henry anyway—"

"You mean Peter John.""All right. Have it your own way. I'll go over to his room and look him up anyway. Good-bye, Phelps."

"Good-bye," responded Will, as the senior started down the stairway.

Several days elapsed before Will heard anything of Wagner's interview with Peter John and then all that Wagner told him was that the freshman had promised faithfully to do better. But Will had already had so much experience with Peter John's promises that he was somewhat skeptical as to results. His classmate he knew was not essentially vicious, only weak. He was so weak and vain that he was eager to gain the favor of whatever person he chanced to be with, and his promise of better things to Wagner was as readily given as was his response to Mott when the latter happened to be his companion of the hour.

Troubled as Will was, he nevertheless did for Peter John all that was within his power, which was not much, and was heavy-hearted as the reports steadily came of his classmate's downfall. Even Hawley, good-natured as he was, had at last rebelled and declared that he would no longer room with a fellow who had no more sense than Schenck, and Peter John, left to himself, was quick to respond to Mott's invitation to share his room, and was soon domiciled in the sophomore's more luxurious quarters.

Will Phelps found meanwhile that his own work in the classroom was of a character that promised a fair grade, though by no means a high one. Even his professor of Greek now appeared in a slightly more favorable light, and Will was convinced that the change was in Splinter, not in himself, so natural and strong were his boyish prejudices.

As the springtime drew near, however, his thoughts and time were somewhat divided in the excitement of the last great struggle between the members of his own class and their rivals, the sophomores. For years it had been the custom of the college for the two lower classes to bury, or rather to burn the hatchet on St. Patrick's Day. For a week preceding that time the tussles between the rival classes were keener than at any other time during the year.

At that eventful date the freshmen for the first time were permitted to carry canes, and on the day itself there was to be a parade of the freshman class, every member clad in some outlandish garment which he wore outside his other clothing, and it was the one ambition of the sophomore class to silence the music of the band that was at the head of the procession and at the same time tear the outer garments from the noisy freshmen. For a week preceding the time of the parade the freshmen were striving by every means in their power to smuggle their canes into Winthrop so that they would all be supplied when the day of emancipation arrived, and the test of the sophomores' keenness was in being able to thwart the plans of their adversaries and prevent the entrance of the canes into the town.

Every road leading to the village was strictly guarded by the vigilant sophomores and spies were busy in the adjacent towns who were continually on the lookout for the purchase or purchasers of the canes. The excitement had become keener with the passing of the days until now only two days remained before the great parade when the huge wooden hatchet would be borne at the head of the procession and duly consigned to the flames on the lower campus in the presence of the entire student body.

Will and Foster had shared in the growing interest and both knew just where the coveted canes had been purchased by the duly authorized committee and hidden till the time should arrive when they were to be brought stealthily into the village. Their excitement became keener still when on the evening of the day to which reference has been made Peter John Schenck burst into Will's room with a report that instantly aroused his two friends.

CHAPTER XXIII

THE RUSH TO COVENTRY CENTER

"The sophs have found out where the canes are," Peter John almost shouted.

"They have? How do you know?" demanded Will.

"I was in my bedroom and I heard them talking with Mott in our study room."

"Who?"

"Tucker, Spencer, and Goodman."

"What did they say?"

"They said the canes were over in Coventry Center, at the minister's house there."

Coventry Center was a little hamlet about seven miles distant from Winthrop, and the excited freshmen had indeed stored a part of their canes in the house of the worthy old minister of the village. They had frankly explained to him what their purpose was and he had laughingly consented to receive the coveted possessions in his home and store them there for the four days that intervened between the time and St. Patrick's day. And the freshmen had been confident that their hiding-place would not readily be discovered. No one would suspect that the parsonage would be selected or the worthy minister would act as a guard. To make assurance doubly certain, however, only half of the canes had been entrusted to the minister, and even those were divided—a bundle containing a dozen being placed in the woodshed and the remaining being stored beneath the hay in the little loft of the barn. The other half of the class canes had been taken to a farmhouse a mile distant from the parsonage and there concealed in an unused well, the mouth of which was filled with rubbish and thedébris of a shed that had been blown down by a severe windstorm that had occurred a few weeks before this time.

As the utmost care had been observed by the committee having in charge the purchase of the canes, and they had stealthily in a stormy night taken their precious burdens to the two places of concealment they had been confident, over-confident now it appeared, that their actions had not been discovered.

Will and Foster had both served on the committee that had purchased and hidden the canes, and when Peter John brought his unwelcome tidings that the rival class was aware of the place where the canes had been stored, it was difficult for them to determine whether anger or chagrin was uppermost in their feelings. At all events they both were greatly excited, and Will said as he hastily rose from his chair:

"How did they find it out?"

"I don't know. I didn't hear them say," replied Peter John.

"Did they find out that you were there?"

"No, they left before I came out of my room. The door was partly open and I didn't dare stir hand or foot."

"Lucky for you, Peter John."

"Yes. I know it.""What are they going to do?" inquired Foster, who up to this time had been silent.

"They've gone over to get the canes."

"Gone!" exclaimed Will aghast.

"Yes. That's what Goodman said."

"How many went, do you know, Peter John?" demanded Foster.

"He said three."

"Do you know who they were?"

"No."

"When did they start?"

"Goodman said they went about an hour ago."

"Which road?"

"I don't know."

"Why didn't Mott go?"

"I don't think he knew anything about it before these fellows came and told him."

"What did he do after they told him?"

"He slapped his legs and laughed."

"You say he went away with those fellows that told him about it?"

"Yes."

"Did they say anything about any other canes—" began Will. But he was sharply interrupted by Foster and abruptly ceased.

"I didn't know there were any others," said Peter John. "Are there? Where are they?"

"We haven't any time to waste here," said Foster, hastily donning his sweater and putting a cap on his head. "Peter John, you go back to your room, and if you hear of anything more go straight to Bishop with the word."

"I'd rather go with you fellows.""Not this trip. You'll have to be on the lookout here. Somebody must do it and you're the one, Peter John. Come on, Will," he added, calling to his room-mate and instantly departed from the room.

Ignoring Peter John, Will hastily followed Foster, and together the two freshmen ran to Hawley's room. There a hurried consultation was held, the result of which was that it was decided that Foster and Dana should secure a car and drive swiftly to Coventry Center by one road, two other classmates were to drive to the same destination by another road, while Will and Hawley were to go on foot across the country and strive to arrive at the minister's house by the time the others had done so. In this way it was believed that every avenue of approach or retreat would be covered, and that even if the sophomores had been first on the scene they would still be unable to get away with their booty before they would be discovered, and at least followed.

In a brief time Will and Hawley were on their way across the country, leaving their more fortunate comrades, who were to ride, to follow as soon as their conveyances could be secured. The ground was still frozen, and in places there were patches of snow and ice, although the heavy snowfall of the winter for the most part was gone. Their way led through woods and over plowed fields, but the steady run or "trot" was maintained uphill and down, and within an hour and a half from the time they had departed from Winthrop they arrived at the confines of the little hamlet of Coventry Center.

"See or hear anything, Will?" inquired Hawley, as the two freshmen stopped and listened intently as they peered all about them.

"Not a thing," whispered Will in response.

The lights in the little homes were already out, for the people of Coventry Center were not believers in keeping untimely hours, and the twinkling lights of the little village for the most part disappeared before ten o'clock arrived. It was about that hour when Will Phelps and Hawley stopped at the end of the one straggling street to try to discover if there were any signs of the presence of their enemies or classmates.

"Shall we wait or put straight for the minister's house?" inquired Hawley.

"Go there," replied Will.

"Look out! Don't let any one see you," said Hawley in a low voice as they stealthily began to make their way up the street. Occasionally they stopped to make sure that they were not being followed or to strive to discover if their own friends were near. They had passed the little white wooden church building and were approaching the parsonage when both stopped abruptly.

"What's that?" demanded Hawley in a whisper.

"You know as much about it as I do. Come on and we'll find out."

The sound of voices could be heard from the rear of the house and from the tones it was evident that the speakers were somewhat excited. Furthermore Will was positive that he recognized the voices of two and they were members of the sophomore class at Winthrop.

"How many are there?" whispered Hawley."Sounds as if there were six or eight. Hark! There's the minister talking."

"What's he saying?"

"I can't make out. He's excited over something, though."

"Come on," whispered Hawley, "let's creep up around the corner of the barn. We can see and hear too there, and if we're careful they won't suspect us."

"It will be all day with us if they do," whispered Will in response.

Slowly and cautiously the two freshmen crept along the side of the street and diagonally across the vacant field till they had gained the desired corner of the barn. Then crouching low they peered forth at the sight which could be seen in the dim light.

On the highest step of the rear piazza of his house stood Mr. Whitaker, the minister of Coventry Center. He was a man at least sixty-five years of age, genial and shrewd, the friend of every one in the region. On the ground before him now five men could be seen and neither Will nor Hawley had any difficulty in recognizing all five as sophomores. Will pinched Hawley's arm in his excitement, but did not speak, though it almost seemed to him that the thumpings of his heart must betray his presence to the men who were before him.

Mr. Whitaker was speaking and instantly Will's attention was centered upon what was being said. "No, young gentlemen, I am not willing that you should enter my house."

"But, Mr. Whitaker," said one in reply whom Will took to be a sophomore who roomed near him in Perry Hall, "we don't want to come into the house—just into the woodshed, that's all."

"I cannot consent even to that."

"We'll not harm anything."

"You certainly will not if you do not enter."

"We've got to come in, Mr. Whitaker!" said the speaker a little more boldly.

"And I forbid it."

An interval in the conversation then followed during which Will could see that the sophomores were conferring. They had withdrawn to a place about midway between the house and the barn and consequently were nearer the hiding-place of the two freshmen than before, but both were compelled to draw back for fear of being discovered and consequently were unable to hear what was said.

In a brief time the sophomores returned to the piazza where the minister was still standing. "Mr. Whitaker," began the leader.

"Yes, sir. At your service," responded the minister pleasantly.

"Why do you object to our coming in? You know we won't do any harm to the place. You know what we've come for."

"Perhaps that's the very reason why I object."

"You don't have to stay here. We'll give you our word we won't harm anything. All we want is to get those freshmen canes. You're not responsible for them and you certainly don't mean to say that you would stand up for that class. Why it's the worst that ever entered Winthrop."

"I have frequently heard of the class," said the minister laughing genially as he spoke. "I have a grandson who chances to be a member of it."

"I beg your pardon. I didn't mean to say that every fellow in it was a poor stick. All I meant was that as a class it's the most conceited one that was ever seen. That's what every one says."

"Doubtless," remarked Mr. Whitaker dryly.

"You don't care anything about the squabbles of the classes. It's nothing to you anyway, Mr. Whitaker," pleaded the sophomore.

"What led you to suspect that the canes might be here?"

"It wouldn't be fair to tell that," laughed the sophomore. "We know they're here all right, and that's enough."

"Would you believe me if I were to say to you that they are not here?"

"Yes, sir, I suppose we should," replied the sophomore dubiously, "but you won't say it."

"Why not, since they are not here?"

"What?" demanded the entire party almost together.

"That is what I said. The canes are not in my house."

"In the barn, then?" said the leader suspiciously.

"No, they are not in the barn, either. There is not a cane on my place except the one I occasionally use myself. If you think that will do—"

"But, Mr. Whitaker, the man was seen when he brought the canes here."

"Quite likely."

"And yet you say they are not here?"

"That is what I said. And what I still say.""I don't understand—"

"I do not say they were not here. All I say is that they are not here."

"They're gone? They've been taken away? Is that what you mean?" demanded the astonished sophomore.

"Precisely."

"Let's go in and search anyway," said one of the party now thoroughly angry.

"I advise you not to attempt that," said the minister quietly.

"Why not?" said the sophomore impudently.

"Because one of my neighbors is a deputy sheriff and housebreaking is a somewhat serious offense."

For a moment the assembly was nonplussed, but their uncertainty was speedily relieved, or at least interrupted, by an occurrence that instantly caused them all to turn and flee from the place at their utmost speed.

CHAPTER XXIV

THE MYSTERY OF THE CANES

At the very moment when the consternation of the sophomores was keenest the sound of a sleigh turning into the yard in which they were standing caused them all to look quickly toward the gateway. The ground was bare in places, and the runners of the sleigh, as the iron bands passed over the gravel, emitted shrieks and groans as if they were striving to warn the sophomores of the impending peril.

Seated in the sleigh were three men whom the assembly speedily recognized as members of the freshman class, and their own fears for a moment doubtless caused the sophomores to magnify the numbers as well as the danger.

"Look out, fellows! Here they come!" said one in a low voice whom Will and Hawley recognized. It was Mott, who was again the spokesman and leader of the little band.

"Let's get out of this," responded one whose voice Will could not determine, and as if a sudden panic had seized upon them the young men turned and began to run swiftly.

"Hold on! Hold on, fellows!" called Mott savagely, although his voice was not loud. "Hold on! What are you running for? There are only three of them, and we're good for any three freshmen in Winthrop. Don't run. Come on back!"

Mott's appeal served to restore a measure of confidence among his companions, and instantly the flight was abandoned and all turned slowly back toward the yard. Neither Will nor Hawley had yet moved from his hiding-place, though they were leaning farther out from the corner of the barn in their eagerness to discover what was occurring in the yard before them. They could see that the driver in the sleigh was Foster, and he had leaped out and was now as calmly tying his horse and fastening the blanket upon it as if never a thought of his rival class had entered his mind. Beside him two young men were standing, but in the dim light it was impossible to determine just who they were. The returning sophomores were now near the new arrivals, and the genial old minister could also be seen, still standing on the piazza and evidently not uninterested in the sight and presence of the young men before him.

"What are you doing here, Bennett?" demanded Mott of Foster.

"Oh, we're out for a sleigh ride," responded Foster glibly, "and we just stopped here to see the fun. What are you doing here?"

"Oh, we stopped to see the fun too," responded Mott gruffly. "It's worth going miles to see freshmen who don't know any more than to go sleigh-riding on bare ground. Had a good time, freshman?"

"Yes. Have you?"

"We're all right. If you've come for the canes you're too late."

"Have you just found that out?" replied Foster with a loud laugh. It was true that he was not aware that the canes had been taken away, but he was not minded to betray his surprise to the members of the rival class.

There was a brief interval of silence which was broken by the old minister, who said, "I shall be very glad, young gentlemen, to have you come into the house. The night air is cold and you must be thoroughly chilled. A little while ago I may have appeared somewhat lacking in hospitality," he added, turning to Mott as he spoke; "but now I can assure you I shall be very glad indeed to receive you."

"Thank you," responded Foster. "We shall be glad to come in if the others will come too."

"We can't very well to-night," said Mott glumly. "We've got to go—"

Suddenly there broke in a wild yell upon the silence of the night. The sound was made by only two men, but these two were possessed of a lung power that was well-nigh phenomenal. Hawley who with his companion had been watching the events that were occurring before them had suddenly turned to Will and whispered, "Let's go in and take a hand! Yell, Phelps! Make them hear you clear over in Winthrop!"

"Hi-i-i-i!" the two lusty freshmen had shouted together as they leaped forward, and the prolonged yell was repeated when all the assembly had instantly turned and for a moment in sheer astonishment were gazing at the startling approach of men from behind the barn.

"Come on, fellows!" shouted Hawley again. "Come on! We'll get every one of them! Come on! Come on!"To the startled sophomores it seemed as if myriads of their foes were rushing upon them, and after a momentary confusion every one had started swiftly across the narrow field that intervened between the yard and the road that approached Coventry Center from another direction.

"Come on, Foster! Come on all you fellows!" shouted Hawley. "Come on! We'll get every soph that's here and will put 'em where they won't do any harm till long after St. Patrick's Day."

Obediently every freshman started to follow Hawley, and across the rough, plowed field they ran swiftly toward the road where the sophomores had already disappeared from sight behind the bushes that were thick and high by the roadside. When once they had gained the road they could see the forms of two men speeding away in the distance, and with a renewed shout the freshmen started in swift pursuit.

On up the long hill they sped until at last they stood together on the summit. Not a sight of their rivals was to be seen, and blankly the freshmen stood and stared about them till Hawley said:

"No use, fellows. They've got away and we might as well go back. Foster," he added, "did you know the canes were gone?"

"Gone? Gone where?" replied Foster blankly.

"I haven't the slightest idea. All I know is that Mr. Whitaker told Mott that the canes had been in his house but they had been taken away."

"Who took them?"

"I haven't the slightest idea.""You don't suppose the sophs got them, do you?" said Foster hastily.

"I hadn't thought of that. It never entered my mind that anybody but our own fellows had come for them."

"I don't believe it was anybody else that got them," said Will. "You ought to have heard Mr. Whitaker talk to Mott and the other sophs. They were just determined to go into his house, but the old man would not let them. No, you can rest easy about it, Mr. Whitaker never let the canes go out of his house without knowing who had come for them. No, sir. Not much."

Somewhat comforted by Will's positiveness, the boys began to retrace their way down the long road, and after a moment Hawley said, "We'll find out all about it anyway, for Mr. Whitaker will tell us. He's all on our side. That's what comes of having his grandson in our class. Say, fellows, you just ought to have heard Mott rake over our class. He had the nerve to stand there and tell Mr. Whitaker that we were the worst lot that had ever entered Winthrop."

"I wish we had caught him!" said Foster warmly. "We would have made him come up in his estimate of the freshmen."

"Oh, he was just talking to hear himself," said Will Phelps lightly. "He knows who we are all right enough, and he isn't going to forget us right away either. But I wish we had caught him."

"Here we are, fellows," said Hawley, as the five young men clambered over the fence and once more were in Mr. Whitaker's yard. "Let's go in and ask him about it now.""All right," responded Foster as they started toward the door. "Hold on a minute. Let me take a look at my horse first. I'll be with you in a minute. Gre-a-at—" he suddenly began. "The horse is gone!"

"What!" exclaimed Will in astonishment.

No heed was given his expression, however, as all five ran quickly to the post to which the horse had been tied. But the horse and sleigh were gone, and not a trace remained to show in which direction they had departed.

"Sure you fastened him all right?" inquired Hawley anxiously.

"I know I did," replied Foster.

"If you did then he couldn't have got loose. I wonder if Mott and the sophs could have done it? Come on! We'll go in and tell Mr. Whitaker and he may be able to give us a point or two. There's a light in the kitchen, and we'll probably find him there. Come on, fellows!"

Hastily the boys ran to the kitchen door, and in response to their knock Mr. Whitaker himself opened the door and stood before them.

"Mr. Whitaker," began Foster, "do you know who took our horse and sleigh?"

"Why! Why, I supposed that you did. Two young men came into the yard not more than three minutes ago and took them away."

"They did? Then it was the sophs," said Foster turning to his comrades. "We'll never hear the last of it. We can't get a horse here, can we, Mr. Whitaker?" he inquired eagerly."I fear not. I have none of my own, and there are not many to be had here anyway."

"Did they start toward Winthrop?"

"I think so. They turned toward the lower road."

"Let's get after them," suggested Foster.

"A long way after them," said Will grimly. "We never could catch up with them."

"Mr. Whitaker," said Hawley, "how long ago were the canes taken away from here?"

The good man hesitated, and the freshman without waiting for him to speak began again. "We belong to the same class as your grandson. We're freshmen and we don't want the sophs to get those canes."

"I regret exceedingly that I had anything to do with it, but my grandson over-persuaded me and so I consented. I should say that it was about an hour ago when they came for the canes."

"Who came?"

"There were two young gentlemen, and they brought me a note which informed me that I was to let them take the canes away."

"A note?" demanded Hawley. "What did it say? Who signed it?"

"It was signed by Hawley—Albert Hawley, if I recollect aright, and also by my grandson."

"My name is Hawley and somebody forged it. The sophs have the canes and I'm afraid it's too late—"

"Too late nothing, Hawley!" said Will impulsively. "What kind of a rig, I mean wagon or sleigh or whatever it was, did they have?" he inquired of the minister."It was a box wagon, a farm wagon, and they had a farmer to drive for them."

"Did you know the man?" demanded Will.

"No. I cannot say that I did. He was a stranger to me. But the note—"

"Probably some soph disguised as a farmer. Did he have any other load in the wagon box?"

"Yes. I noticed some bags of meal."

"Good. And you say they took the lower road?"

"Yes. I recollect that distinctly."

"Isn't there a short cut? Can't we cut across lots and head them off? They would have to go slow, and it might be that we could head them somewhere and get those canes away from them."

"Yes," replied Mr. Whitaker. "I don't know that I am doing right to tell you, but inasmuch as the canes were secured by a forgery I shall certainly tell you all I know of the matter. If you go down to that little valley," and as he spoke he pointed in a direction in the rear of the barn, "you will find a pathway that leads beside the brook almost in a straight line to what we call the ford. It saves between three and four miles to Winthrop, and whenever I walk I take the path. I—"

"Thank you! Thank you, Mr. Whitaker! Come on! We'll try it anyway, fellows. We've nothing to lose and everything to gain. Good night, Mr. Whitaker! Thank you for what you've told us," called Will Phelps, as he quickly turned and began to run.

Obediently the boys all followed Will as he ran swiftly across the field, and in a brief time they discovered the pathway to which the old minister had referred. There was no conversation now, for the fear in every heart was that they would arrive at the ford too late to avail. Besides, there was the likelihood that the canes would be disposed of before the wagon had gone very far from Mr. Whitaker's house. A multitude of fears possessed them, but they ran swiftly along the path where Will Phelps, eager and strong was leading the way. Not once did they stop for rest. The night air was chilling, and the clouds that swept across the face of the sky did not hide the light of the moon.

On and on they sped, steadily maintaining the dogged pace which the leader was setting for them, until at last, well-nigh winded and thoroughly tired by their exertions, they arrived at the place where the pathway joined the road and they knew that Winthrop was not more than three-quarters of a mile away. There they halted, but they had not recovered from the effects of their long run when they perceived a farm wagon, apparently filled with bags, coming down the hill that was near them.

CHAPTER XXV

ON THE TRAIL

As the eager freshmen peered out at the approaching wagon the suppressed excitement threatened to break all bounds. "Let's stop him and get the canes," suggested Hawley in a whisper.

"No. What'll be the good of that? It'll be better to follow up the wagon quietly, and then if we can find out where they put the canes, maybe a little later we can get them away without the sophs knowing anything about it. Don't you see we'll be making it all the worse for them."

"We don't know that the canes are in the wagon," suggested Foster.

"Of course we don't, and it's all the same whether we try to find out now or follow it up and find out a little later."

"Phelps is right about it," said Hawley. "If the canes shouldn't be found in the wagon, we would be making fools of ourselves if we stopped it, but if we let it go on and follow it up we'll be all the better."

Meanwhile the wagon itself had passed the place where the boys were concealed, and groaning and creaking had begun the ascent of the opposite hill. Only the driver was to be seen, and his appearance and actions were unmistakable. He was a farmer and well advanced in years, and if he was aware of the contest that was being waged between the rival classes in Winthrop it was evident that he had no share in the excitement.

"How'll we do it, fellows?" inquired Hawley anxiously. "He'll get away before we get our eyes open, if we don't look out."

"Let's follow him," said Will Phelps quickly. "We mustn't go in a bunch, but string out. But we mustn't be so far apart that we can't hear if one of us calls or whistles."

"Come on, then," said Foster. "You go ahead, Will, and we'll come along. You're a runner, and if the old fellow begins to start up his horses you can follow him better than any of us can. But we'll have to do our best."

Quickly the suggestion was adopted, and Will ran swiftly along the road until he discovered the wagon not far in advance of him. It was moving at the same monotonous pace as when it had passed the hiding place of the boys. Will Phelps, when he came within a hundred yards of the wagon he was following, decreased his own speed and endeavored to keep close to the fences by the roadside, so that he would not be seen by the driver if he should chance to look behind him.

They were soon within sight of Winthrop, and the shadowy towers of the college buildings could be discerned in the distance. It was long past midnight, and the only lights that could be seen were those of the twinkling stars and the occasional flash of the moonlight when the broken clouds that were moving across the face of the sky parted sufficiently for the face of the moon to be seen.

Suddenly Will was aware that the wagon had stopped at a corner where a road or street that led to the lower part of the village joined the road that led past the college buildings. He darted behind a huge tree that grew close to the roadside, and eagerly peered forth to discover what the next move of the farmer would be. He could see that some one approached the wagon, and after a brief delay climbed up on the seat beside the driver and then the team started on once more. Will was keenly excited by this time, and his suspicions were confirmed that the canes were indeed in the wagon before him. He was eager to follow swiftly, but he quickly decided that it would be wiser to wait until Hawley came up to the place where he himself was waiting and explain to him the change in the direction of the party they were following.

The huge form of Hawley soon appeared, and impatiently Will ran out into the road to meet him. "They've turned in here," he said excitedly, "and you must stop here and tell the fellows. I'll run on ahead and find out where the wagon goes."

Quickly Will darted across the fields and soon came into the lower road. The wagon could be seen not far in advance of him, and was still moving at a slow pace from which it had not varied since it first had been seen. It was evident that the sophs were either indifferent or absolutely confident, Will could not determine which. For a moment his heart misgave him. What a plight he would be in if it should appear that he and his classmates had been following a purposely designed trick of their rivals. The thought was by no means reassuring, but there was no time afforded for reflection, for the wagon he was following even then turned into a lane that led to a farmhouse and barns that were not far from the road. The climax had almost been reached and it would be soon known what the issue was to be.

Will waited now for his classmates to join him. The wagon could not escape, for the lane came to an abrupt end in the yard, and if it should turn back it could not pass the place where he was waiting without being seen.

It was not long before Hawley joined him, and, as he approached, Will said: "They've gone down this lane. Somebody was waiting here and has gone with the driver. There may be a good many others down there by the barn for all that we know. What do you think we'd better do?"

"There's a haystack out there by the barn," said Hawley, pointing to a stack of some kind that could be seen in the rear of the nearest barn. "If you could only get behind that you could see what was going on."

"I can, all right enough. But where will you fellows be? I may need your help if I get into trouble."

"I don't know. We won't be far away. Whistle if you want us and we'll make a break for you. Don't let them see you," he added warningly, as without waiting to reply, Will started at once, running swiftly along the ground near the crooked rail fence that extended the entire distance between the main road and the farm buildings.

He was convinced that he had not been seen when at last he gained the shelter of the haystack, and, crouching within its shadows, he peered forth at the wagon and the group of four men that were standing near it. He was positive that one was Mott, but his greatest surprise came when he perceived a horse and sleigh in the barnyard which he instantly recognized as the very ones with which Foster and his two classmates had gone to Coventry Center. He reached forward and strove to hear what was being said, for the little group were conversing eagerly but in tones so low that Will was unable to hear a word. He could see what was done, however, for after a brief delay the four men turned to the wagon, several sacks were lifted from their places in the load, and then two other sacks were taken from the wagon and carried by Mott and another man into the barn. Several minutes elapsed before Mott came forth again, and when he did he was alone. The sophomore stopped for a moment with the men, handed some money to the farmer, and then he and the fourth man, whom Will fancied he recognized as another sophomore, climbed into the sleigh and at once started back up the lane, the runners of the sleigh screeching as they passed over the bare places as if they were doing their utmost to alarm the neighborhood and to protest against what was being done. The farmer too, soon followed and passed up the lane, but his departure was of slight interest to Will, who was puzzling himself about the man who had entered the barn with Mott and had failed to reappear. To Will's mind there was but one explanation, and he was eager to confer with his own classmates, but he dared not leave his hiding-place for fear that the man in the barn might come forth and depart without being seen.

For a half-hour he waited but the stillness of the night was unbroken. He was becoming chilled and he dared not remain longer where he was. At last he decided to return to the place where he had left his own classmates and report to them what he had seen.

Hastily withdrawing from his shelter he ran swiftly across the fields until he came to the corner, and then whistling softly was rejoiced when he perceived his friends rise from the ground in an angle of the crooked fence and advance to meet him.

"Is that you, Will?" said Foster in a low voice. "We didn't know what had become of you. What's up? What's wrong?"

Will hastily described what he had seen and then said, "I'm dead sure, fellows, that that soph has been left in the barn to watch those canes."

"Why didn't you run away with the horse and sleigh?" inquired Hawley.

"I did think of trying it. But I made up my mind that even if I should succeed in doing it, it would give the whole thing away. They'd know that we'd found out where they had hidden our canes and there wouldn't be much use in our trying to get them again. Now we know where they are and the sophs don't even know that we know."

"You mean you think they don't know that we know," suggested Foster."I know it!" asserted Will positively. "Now what shall we do?"

"Put straight back to the barn, tie up the soph and take the canes away with us," said Hawley promptly.

"I've thought of that," replied Will. "But do you think that's the best plan? If we take the canes away we may lose them, for St. Patrick's Day isn't till day after to-morrow, you know. If this soph, I don't know who he is, has been left as guard he'll be relieved, and if they find he's gone and the canes too, why it'll be all the harder for us."

"What do you suggest, Phelps?" inquired Hawley.

"How will this do? Some one of us can creep back there into the barn and keep watch the same as the soph is doing. He can be relieved in the morning and then some one else can take his place. If anything happens in the barn he'll be pretty likely to know it, and if anything doesn't happen then we can get up a good-sized crowd and go down there to-morrow night and get the canes. We can distribute them among our fellows and then the next morning every fellow in the class can march into chapel with his cane."

"Good! Good! That's the idea!" said Hawley warmly. "Who'll go down in the barn and be guard for the night?"

"Who's got the most cuts to spare?" inquired Will.

"I have," said Foster promptly. "I have taken but four.""Then I should say you were the one to stand guard to-morrow," said Will. "I'll go to-night myself," he added. "Come down just before it's light in the morning, and come to the door in the rear of the barn. Rap three times softly, and then if that doesn't work, whistle, but not too loud."

There was some demurring on the part of his classmates, each of whom demanded for himself the privilege of taking the first watch, but Will insisted, and then somewhat reluctantly he was left to make his way back to the barn and all the others soon returned to the dormitories.

When Will Phelps arrived at the rear door of the barn he discovered that it was locked on the inside and he was unable to gain an entrance there. He was fearful that to enter by the front door would be but to proclaim his presence, but at last he perceived that there was an entrance by a small door that was partly open above the roof of the little lean-to on the side of the barn. Carefully he climbed up on the roof and cautiously made his way to the door. He peered within but it was dark and at first he was unable to discern anything. He waited until his eyes became somewhat accustomed to the dim light and then saw that there was a bare floor before him and that adjoining it was the haymow.

With his utmost care he stepped inside, and his fears increased when he discovered that the loose flooring creaked and groaned beneath his feet. With every step he halted and listened intently. It seemed to the excited freshman that he never had heard such sounds as those boards emitted that night. So slowly and cautiously did he proceed that it seemed to him that hours must have elapsed before he succeeded in gaining the border of the low mow. Even then he halted and listened intently, but not a sound broke in upon the oppressive stillness that pervaded the barn.

He next carefully and cautiously stepped over into the mow. A faint glimmer of light came from one corner and there he concluded the ladder must be which led to the floor below. If he could gain a place near that, he assured himself he would be able to know if anything occurred below, and at the same time he himself would be secure from observation.

Once more he slowly and with the utmost care began to creep forward, and at last he stretched himself at full length upon the hay and peered down through the opening. It was too dark to permit him to see much and not a sound could be heard.

Satisfied that he had been successful he resigned himself to his watch. The long hours dragged on until at last Will found it almost impossible to keep himself awake. Desperately he strove to keep his eyes open, but his feeling of drowsiness increased until at last it overpowered him and the weary freshman was fast asleep.

He was rudely awakened by sounds that came from the room below. He sat quickly erect, and though the light was clearer now he at first could not collect his thoughts sufficiently to show him where he was. Quickly, however, as the sounds from below became louder, it all came back to him, and he ran to the ladder and peered through the opening. What he saw evidently startled him, for instantly he threw himself upon the ladder and almost leaped to the floor below.

CHAPTER XXVI

ST. PATRICK'S DAY

The door in the rear of the barn was open and on the floor before it stood Foster and Mott facing each other. Whether or not the sophomore who had been left as a guard was still in the barn Will could not determine, but, without waiting to find out, he almost leaped to the floor below, and before Mott could recover from his surprise he was helpless in the hands of his enemies. It was but the work of a moment securely to bind his hands and feet, and the leading spirit of the sophomore class was soon a helpless captive.

Excited though the boys were, the entire adventure was completed in a very brief time, and Will and Foster were both laughing when they gazed at their helpless prisoner. Even Mott smiled as he said ruefully:

"You've scored, freshmen. What are you going to do with me?"

"Nothing," said Will quickly.

Mott drew down the corners of his mouth and then a sudden light appeared in his eyes that caused Will to look keenly at him for a moment. "Come on, Foster," he said simply; "let's put this fellow where he won't do any more harm, at least until after St. Patrick's Day."

"Where'll we put him?" inquired Foster.

Will turned and looked about him and perceived a small harness room on the ground floor near him, and upon his suggestion the helpless sophomore was placed within it for safe keeping.

"Now then, Foster," said Will when he had closed the door of the room, "we've just got to find the place where these canes are hidden. Mott has come here to take the place of the guard that was here last night and nobody knows how long it'll be before some one else comes. Come on, let's get about it."

At once the two freshmen began their search. Beginning near the entrance, they examined every bin and peered into every possible place of concealment. Even in the mangers before which the horses were tied they peered and searched, but when they had carefully examined the entire floor they had not been able to discover the place where the coveted canes had been concealed.

"What are we to do, Will?" demanded Foster at last.

"Let's ask Mott."

"He'll never let on."

"Try it, anyway."

The two boys returned to the harness room and Will at once addressed their prisoner.

"Mott," he said, "where are those canes?"

The sophomore laughed loudly as he replied, "You certainly are the two most innocent freshmen I have ever struck yet. Perhaps you'd like to have me help you carry them back to the college."

"We'll let you go if you'll tell us where they are."

"Thanks muchly," replied Mott dryly."Come on, Will," said Foster. "We can find them ourselves. No use in wasting time here with this fellow. We'll get them ourselves."

"You're certain they're here?" laughed Mott.

Neither responded to his question, but both left the room and resumed their search.

"You don't suppose they have really got those canes somewhere else, do you, Foster? They might be just trying to put us on the wrong track here, you know?" inquired Will.

"It's possible, but I don't believe it," said Foster positively. "If that was their game Mott wouldn't be here."

"Probably not," assented Will. "Let's begin again. We've no time to waste."

The freshmen now began to search in the loft of the barn. They seized the pitchforks that were in the mow, and, thrusting the tines into the hay, they continued their search, working with desperate determination and throwing the hay about them until the entire mow presented the appearance of having been almost completely overturned.

But not a trace of the missing canes could they discover. At last, satisfied that their efforts were vain, they ceased and for a moment stared blankly at each other.

"No use," said Will despondently. "They've made game of us this time, Foster, just as sure as you live."

"We won't give up yet, Will. Of course if the canes are here they were not put where we'd be likely to stumble over them. We've just got to think it out—"

Foster stopped abruptly as a voice was heard calling up from below. "I must bid you an affectionate and tearful farewell, freshmen. Keep on with your good work and remember that perseverance conquers everything. Even the best of friends must part—"

Foster and Will waited to hear no more, but both plunged down the ladder, but when they had gained the floor below it was to behold Mott speeding up the lane as if he was "sprinting" for life itself. For a moment the surprise and consternation of the two freshmen were so complete that both were speechless.

"Why didn't you take after him, Will?" said Foster, who was the first to break in upon the awkward silence. "What are you standing here for?"

"No use, Foster," replied Will, shaking his head. "He's got too good a start. I don't see how he ever got loose."

"Well, he is loose and that's all there is about it. What'll we do next?"

"Find those canes. They're here, I know they are."

"Just tell me where they are, will you?"

"They won't come to us, that's certain! We've got to look them up. And if we don't find them pretty soon too it'll be the worse for us."

Will turned as he spoke and once more opened the lid of a piano box that was standing on the floor near them. The box apparently was filled with oats and they had inspected it before, but as it had not presented any appearance of containing the object of their search they had passed it by and gone on to the loft above.

This time, however, Will thrust his arm deep down into the oats and in a moment he almost shouted. "Here's something, Foster! Help me clear away these oats. There's something down in there!"

Foster seized the scoop that was near the improvised oat bin and with feverish haste threw the oats up on one side and then said exultantly, "Here's something! Here they are!"

Leaning over the box, he drew forth a bundle of canes carefully tied together and partly hidden from sight beneath the oats.

"Are they all there?" demanded Will in a hoarse whisper. He hastily inspected the bundle and then exclaimed, "Here's only a part of them, Foster!"

"Where some are it's likely there are more," and Will at once resumed his search. His efforts were speedily rewarded by the discovery of another bundle similar to the one that had already been found, and, dropping his scoop, he hastily began to count the canes.

"Here they are!" he exclaimed joyfully. "Every last one of them is here!"

"Then the sophs must have been to both places where we had them."

"Yes, but it's all the better for us. We'll now be—"

Foster stopped abruptly as the farmer that owned the buildings appeared in the doorway and for a moment stared blankly at them.

"Good morning," said Will cheerfully. "We're here after these canes."

"So I see," replied the farmer. "The freshmans didn't find ye out, then?"

"It's all right," responded Will glibly. "How much are we to pay you?"

"They paid me last night. I guess 'twas 'beout right. I don't want nothin' more."

"We've tumbled your hay over more than we thought," said Will, as he thrust a bill into the man's hand.

"I don't know 'beout it," drawled the farmer, nevertheless thrusting the money into his pocket. "Putty good pay, but I don't know but I might's well take it."

"Of course you're to take it!" said Will eagerly. "All we ask of you now is not to tell anybody—anybody," he added with special emphasis, "that we've taken the canes away. Don't tell any one of it or the whole game will be spoiled."

"I'll be as mum as a hitchin' post."

Without waiting for any further words the two boys seized the bundles and at once departed from the barn. When they came out into the lane they looked carefully about them in every direction, but no one could be seen and they soon came out into the open road.

"What are we going to do with them now?" inquired Foster, as they halted for a moment."We can't take them back to our rooms," said Will.

"No! No! That would never do."

"I'll tell you," said Will quickly. "Let's take them down to that old bridge yonder," pointing as he spoke toward a rude bridge that spanned the stream not far away.

"All right. Come along, then," responded Foster.

Instantly the two boys began to run and in a brief time arrived at the rude structure, and after a hasty inspection they placed the two bundles on the piers beneath the bridge and then covered them with the driftwood that had been cast up on the bank of the stream when its waters had been swelled by the passing storms.

When their work was at last completed they departed for Winthrop and arrived just as the final strokes of the bell were given that assembled the students in the chapel. They hastily passed in with the throng of students and were in their seats in time to receive credit for attendance.

As they passed out from the chapel when the service was ended they came face to face with Mott and a group of sophomores, who evidently were waiting for their appearance; but as neither Foster nor Will betrayed any emotion by the expression upon their faces it was impossible for the sophomores to perceive whether or not the canes had been discovered.

There was no question about their opinions, however, when later in the day it was apparent that the sophomore class was possessed of a feeling of intense excitement. Parties were sent forth in various directions, and there was the keenest interest manifest in the entire college. Will and Foster, however, were too wise to relate their experiences to any except to the three or four leaders of their class; and when night fell, by a circuitous route, and then only after a half-dozen parties had been sent out in other directions to mislead any of their rivals who might be watching their movements, they proceeded to the bridge, secured the canes, and bringing them safely back to the college under the protecting shelter of the darkness, distributed them among the members of the class.

Great was the elation of the freshmen when on the following morning they formed in a body near the gymnasium just before the hour of morning prayers in the chapel and then marched to the service every one carrying in his hands one of the coveted sticks.

The discomfited sophomores endured in silence the gibes of the students, and the exultant freshmen received the applause that greeted their success with an air that it is to be feared only served to increase the chagrin of their rivals. And Will Phelps and Foster were at once, and by a common though unspoken assent, awarded a place among the leaders of their class for their success.

Of the parade that took place that day Will Phelps did not tire of talking for many a week. The assembled crowd of students, townspeople, and visitors, the long line of freshmen in the parade and their grotesque appearance, the stirring music of a brass band at the head of the line, the march to the lower campus where the huge bonfire was kindled, the weird songs and dancing as in dual lines the two lower classes with joined hands leaped and danced about the blazing fire, and then the final consignment to the flames of the huge wooden hatchet that had been carried in the parade, were all incidents that duly impressed him. And when at last the fires burned low and the final song was sung, and it was declared that the hatchet was buried forever and all feelings of animosity between the lower classmen were at an end, the boys returned to their rooms feeling that a well-earned victory had been won.

The escapades were doubtless silly, and in after years brought a smile to the faces of the participants when they were then recalled, but nevertheless they had formed a part of the experiences of college life and had brought with them the development of certain qualities of leadership which in other ways and in later days were to play no small part in the lives of Will Phelps and his room-mate.

The coming of springtime in Winthrop was always an occasion of general rejoicing. The hills were once more covered with their garments of green and the valleys were beautiful in their verdure. Among the students at Winthrop there was usually a relaxing of effort then, but Will Phelps, though the effort cost him much, still held himself resolutely to his tasks. He had been learning not merely what to study but also how to study, and in his spring vacation his father had explained to him that this was his supreme purpose and desire. If a man did not learn how to work while he was a student in college it was seldom the case that he learned it afterward. And Will had responded. His Greek was still distasteful to him, but he was doing somewhat better and was more content.

The crowning ambition in Will's heart as we know was to secure a place on the college track team. And he had been working quietly yet persistently under the guidance of Wagner for the desired end. At last, early in May, came the trial meets of the college when the selections for the team were to be made, and when Will donned his running suit and went down to the track to all appearances he was calmer than his room-mate. But in his heart there was a feeling such as he had never known before.

CHAPTER XXVII

CONCLUSION

It was a noisy crowd of students that assembled at the Winthrop athletic field on that day early in May when the trials for the track team were to be held. Keen as was the interest in baseball the interest in the track team was even keener, for hope was high among the students that a championship team would be turned out and the competition among the eight colleges that composed the league was at fever heat. The most formidable rival of Winthrop was Alden, and, as within the past four years each of the two colleges had won the championship twice, the coming contest would decide the possession of the cup which the association had voted should be held in the permanent possession of the college which had won most of the meets within the limits of the five years.

Will Phelps was keenly excited although his movements were very deliberate as he walked about the field clad in his running suit, over which he was wearing his bath robe. His desire to secure a place on the team was so strong that he hardly dared face the possibility of a failure. The disappointments of the year would in a measure be atoned for if only he might win the coveted honor. He had carefully followed the instructions of Wagner, the captain of the team, who though, by his physician's orders was not to compete, was nevertheless deeply interested and for some reason had taken an especially strong liking to Will Phelps. Upon his advice Will had retired early the preceding night and had secured a rest that made him now feel that if ever he was to win, the present opportunity was the supreme one.

"Don't do your best in the heats, unless you have to," said Wagner as he approached Will on the field and stopped for a moment to chat with him. "Save your strength for the finals."

Will smiled but did not reply. In his present state of mind he was wondering if he could run at any pace that was not his best. The events were being run off now and he was striving to become interested in them. Anything that would call his thoughts away from himself and his own contest was to be desired, he thought. Foster had tried and failed to win a place and Peter John Schenck too had not been successful. Was his own chance better than theirs? He could hardly believe that it was, and yet if determination could aid he knew that his lack, if he should be found wanting, would not be due to that cause.

At last the supreme moment arrived and the call for the first heat in the hundred yards dash was heard. Will's heart was beating furiously when he cast aside his bath robe and tossed it to Foster who was waiting to receive it. His room-mate smiled encouragingly but was too wise to speak and Will advanced to the line. He perceived that three others were with him in the heat, but Mott, whom he most feared, was not among the number. That was a source of some consolation, and his hope increased that he might at least win a place in the finals.As the pistol was fired, Will darted forward from the line, but in a moment the runners were recalled and Will was penalized a yard for his undue eagerness. Grimly he took his place this time a yard behind the line and when the start was again made he sped down the track as if he was possessed of the speed of the wind. Easily he was the first to touch the tape, but when unmindful of the cheers of his classmates he turned aside to don once more his bath robe, Wagner approached and shaking his head, laughed as he said, "You forgot what I told you, freshman."

"What was that?"

"Not to run your best in the heat. You want something left for the finals."

"I couldn't help it," said Will grimly. "What was the time?"

"Ten, two."

Nothing more was said as they all turned to watch the runners in the other heats. Mott with apparent ease won his, and Ogden won the third. The final was to be run off between the three winners and Will stretched himself upon the grass to gain such rest as he could obtain before the supreme test arrived.

Other events were now run off and a half-hour elapsed before the final heat was called. "You'll get your place on the team anyway, Will," said Foster encouragingly.

"I'm not so sure of that."

"I am. I heard Wagner say that three would be taken on the team for the sprints, and even if you come in last you'll be sure of a place."

"I don't know. I don't want to come in last."

"Don't, then," laughed Foster as he reached forth his hand for his room-mate's bath robe. Once more Will stood on the line and this time there would be no "sneaking," he assured himself. Somehow the keenness of his previous excitement was gone now and he was almost as calm as if he had been a spectator and not a participant in the contest. He was none the less resolved to do his utmost and when the pistol at last was fired he leaped from the mark with every nerve and muscle tense. A silence rested over all as the three runners came swiftly up the track. Will could feel rather than see that he was ahead of Ogden, but Mott was still in advance of him, and do what he might he did not seem to be able to cut down that yard by which Mott was leading. Swiftly the racers sped on and soon Will could see that the end of the course had almost been gained. Only fifteen yards remained to be covered, and then by one supreme effort Will called upon all his reserve powers and with what the college paper afterward described as a "magnificent burst of speed," he cut down Mott's lead and a moment later the two runners struck the tape exactly together.

A mighty shout arose from the assembled students and Foster and Hawley both of whom were usually so self-contained ran out and threw their arms about the neck of their classmate. The enthusiasm increased when the time was announced as "ten, one." and Wagner came forward his face beaming and his hand outstretched as he said: "You did it, freshman! I knew you could, and I knew you would."

Words of praise had never sounded sweeter in Will's ears. He had won a place on the team and that coveted honor at least was his.

His interest in the trials was mostly ended now and he returned to the dressing rooms, where he donned his ordinary garb and then rejoined his fellows. Their congratulations were sweet in his ears and the very appearance of the beautiful valley to him seemed to have changed. He had won and the stimulus of success was his.

In the month that followed Will found himself excessively busy. He took his meals now with the team at the training table and every day there was work to be done on the track. And it was hard work too. But the demands were almost forgotten in the elation which filled the heart of the young student. His father's warm words of congratulation were prized most of all, but Will felt that he did not require the caution which his father gave him not to permit his success in athletics to interfere with his work for the classroom. Even "Splinter's" demands had lost a part of their unreasonableness, or so it seemed to Will, and even the detested Greek could be mastered under the glow of success that was his.

At last the eventful day arrived when the meet between the colleges was to be held. Will had worked so hard and so faithfully that he was not without hopes of winning some points for his college and he was aware how much they were needed and how eager all the student body was that the cup might come to Winthrop. Mott was the only one who had appeared to be at all envious of him, but as Will had heard that the sophomore had been careless in his training and there had been reports that Mott and Peter John had been drinking heavily again, he felt that he could well afford to ignore the slights. And in his heart he knew that he was sincere when he declared to himself that if he could not win he heartily wished that Mott might, for Winthrop would be the gainer in either event.

The team had been taken to the city where the meet was to be held, on the day preceding the contest, and that night at the hotel Will endeavored again to follow the advice of Wagner and secure a good sleep. But his excitement and the novelty of his surroundings and thoughts of the impending meet were too keen to be entirely overcome by the young freshman, and on the following morning his heart was somewhat heavy and his fears increased.

When at last the hour arrived when the team, in a huge coach, was taken to the field, a measure of calm had returned to him and as he looked out over the great assembly his interest became intense. Students from the various colleges had been assigned sections in the bleachers and streamers and banners with the huge initial letter of the college emblazoned upon them were much in evidence. The colors of the competing colleges were also to be seen among the spectators and with shouts and cheers and songs to be heard on every side Will felt that this was the supreme moment of his life. He stood gazing at the inspiring sight until he felt a touch on his shoulder that caused him quickly to turn about.

"Why, pop!" he exclaimed delightedly as he perceived who it was that had touched him. "I didn't have the remotest idea that you were here."

"I had to come to see what my boy would do," replied Mr. Phelps quietly.

"I'm afraid you won't see much."

"I shall see him do his best, and that's worth the trip."

"Come on, freshman!" interrupted Mott approaching. "It's time to dress."

Will grasped his father's hand for a moment and then hastened to follow the other members of the Winthrop team who were making their way to their quarters.

"Alden is going to win all the sprints," said Mott glumly while they were dressing.

"If they're the best runners they will," assented Will who despite his eagerness was now in good spirits.

"Wagner has figured it out and says if they do win the sprints they'll take the cup."

Will made no response though he knew that if Wagner had indeed said that, then the college would look to Mott and to himself to do their best. No praise would be too high if they should succeed, and no blame too severe if they should fail. And his own determination and desire to win for a moment faltered. What could he in his first great contest hope to do?

The appearance of the team on the field was greeted by a wild shout from the Winthrop contingent. The team was cheered and every member of it also was cheered by name. The entire scene was certainly inspiring and Will's determination returned more strongly than before. The first event was the four hundred and forty yard dash in which Alden received first and Winthrop second. In the one hundred and twenty yard hurdles the order was reversed, and so the record continued through the two-twenty, the two-twenty hurdles, the eight hundred and eighty yards run. The field events were also being carried out at the same time and with very similar results. Alden was second in the shot put and Winthrop second in the running high jump while neither scored in throwing the hammer nor in the running broad jump. But again Winthrop was first in throwing the discus, but Alden was first in the pole vault; and so the points scored by each of the two rivals remained the same when at last came the trials in the hundred yards dash, which as we know was the event in which Will Phelps and Mott were entered. The color had fled from Will's face and he was hardly conscious of the shouts or presence of the great assembly when he advanced to the line, for he was to run in the first heat. Thirty-two men were entered for the race and there were to be six heats, only the winners in each to qualify for the finals.

"You've nobody to fear here," whispered Wagner encouragingly. "Take it easy.""I'll have to come in first if I get in the finals."

"Yes, but you can do it all right."

Wagner slipped back and the seven young men took their places on the line. When the pistol was fired Will darted forward and held the lead all the way, touching the tape first of all.

Wagner again was there to receive him and as Will fell into his arms he turned quickly and said. "What was the time?"

"They'll announce it in a minute," replied Wagner compelling his friend to don his robe. When the time was announced as "ten three," Will's heart sank, but Wagner laughed gleefully as he said, "Good! That's the way to do it. You've got some reserve left."

Will Phelps was not so confident, but he turned eagerly to watch the other contestants. Mott won his heat in ten two, each of two heats was won by an Alden man in the same time, and the fifth heat was won by a man from a smaller college of whom no one expected much and who was but slightly feared.

The mile run, the two mile run, and the half-mile were run off while the sprinters were waiting for their finals and the excitement became intense when it was known that the score of Winthrop and Alden was exactly the same. Everything now depended upon the result of the finals in the hundred yards dash.

"Phelps, you must get it!" whispered Wagner whose face was as pale as that of the freshman. Will did not reply and at once took his place beside his four competitors.

"On your marks!" called the starter, and the silence that rested over the field became intense.

"Get set!" A sigh seemed to rise from the assembly and all were standing.

"Go!" The crack of the pistol was heard and instantly the runners were speeding down the track.

The day was warm and Will Phelps could feel that his face was as wet as if he had plunged in the river. Never in all his young life had he exerted himself as then. The tread of the running feet on the track seemed almost like that of one man. On and on they sped, no one looking to the right or left. Whether he was winning or not, Will was unable to determine. He knew that all five were "bunched," for he could feel and hear the others near him. The deafening shouts and the shrill calls and cries sounded faint and dim in his ears. He could see the officials standing near the end of the course—an end that seemed far away for all that the runners were so swiftly approaching.

Nearer and nearer the runners drew and the shouts increased in violence. Every one in the assembly was standing erect and leaning forward, breathless with interest. Fifteen, ten, then only five yards remained. With one supreme effort Will darted ahead. He felt the tape, and not knowing whether he had won or not he plunged into the outstretched arms of Wagner.

For a moment everything was dim about him and there was a sound as of a roaring in his ears. Then above the din he heard the wild shout of the Winthrop boys and he heard Wagner say, "The cup's ours, Phelps! We've got it! We've won it!"

"Was I first?" inquired Will simply.

"No, second."

"I don't see then. Who did win?"

"Crafts from Tech was first and you were second and the Alden man third," said Wagner hilariously. "You put us two points ahead of Alden! You've won your 'W' and we've got the cup!"

Before Will could respond a body of the Winthrop boys made a rush upon him and lifting him upon their shoulders advanced to the middle of the field followed by the entire body of their fellow-students. Then in fantastic steps and winding column they marched about the field, singing their college songs and uniting in their college yell for the team and for Phelps again and again. The interested spectators stopped and watched the proceedings until at last the team returned to their dressing rooms and the day was done.

On the return to Winthrop Will was seated beside his father, and as they drew near the college town Mr. Phelps, who was not to stop, but was at once going home, said: "Well, Will, what of the year? It's done now."

"Yes," responded Will simply. "It's not been so bad."

"What about the Greek?"

"Oh, Splinter's not half-bad either," laughed Will. "I think I'll go down and see him before I come home.""I should. And you're not sorry that you didn't give up to Greek?"

"Not a bit."

"And you think winning the 'hundred' to-day is worth it all?"

"It isn't that. It's the feeling that I haven't given up. Of course I'm glad to get my 'W' and I was mighty sorry not to get my numerals. But this makes up for it. I'm glad I won out for myself and more for the college. I tell you, pop, Winthrop is the best college in the world!"

"And you wouldn't like to leave now?"

"Leave? Well, I guess not!"

"I hear that Peter John is not to come back," said Mr. Phelps soberly.

"Why not?"

"I can't say. I don't even know that he is not to return. I have heard it, that's all; but I fancy you know more about it than I."

Will was silent till the train was near Winthrop. "Well, Will," said his father, breaking in, "I'm to leave you here. Do you want to know what I value most in your year's work?"

"What is it?"

"That you've learned how to work. When a man learns that, much of the problem of his life is solved. Some men run from hardness, some endure it, and some overcome it."

"It hasn't been so hard."

Mr. Phelps smiled but all he said was, "Good-bye, Will, we'll look for you soon at home. I think you've made a good investment this year."

"In what?" inquired Will in surprise.

But his father only smiled and grasped his son's hand for a moment and soon the train pulled out from the little station; but as long as the crowd of students, noisy, boisterous, happy, could be seen as they moved up the street he watched them with shining eyes. Then as he resumed his seat he thoughtfully said to himself, "Yes, Will has learned it. I did not know for a time whether he would or not. But he has and I don't think Splinter, or Mott, or Peter John, or anything, or any one can take it away from him now."

And he resumed the reading of his evening paper, while the noisy train sped on bearing him farther and farther from Winthrop, but the Winthrop college boy was nearer to him all the time.

THE END

Milton Keynes UK
Ingram Content Group UK Ltd.
UKHW040902181023
430840UK00004B/173